"Me too. I don't know what I'd do without you, Katie. Whenever I think about last summer, about how you were so close to dying . . ."

She didn't allow him to complete his sentence. "Every day is new, every morning, Josh. I'm glad I got a second chance at life. And after meeting the people here at Jenny House, after making friends with Amanda, Chelsea, and even Lacey, I want all of us to live forever."

He grinned. "Forever's a long time."

She returned his smile. "All right, then at least until we're all old and wrinkled."

Katie O'Roark knows how lucky she is. She not only was able to find a donor for the heart transplant surgery she needed, she has survived the operation and resumed a normal life.

She knows she owes much of her good fortune to JWC, the anonymous individual from the One Last Wish Foundation. When Katie receives a letter asking her to help the foundation, she readily agrees.

Follow Katie O'Roark, first introduced in *Someone Dies, Someone Lives*, in this new One Last Wish trilogy:

Please Don't Die
She Died Too Young
For All the Days of Her Life

ONE LAST WISH

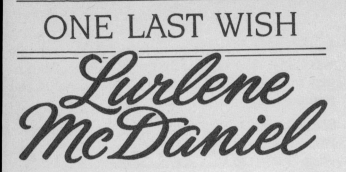

Please Don't Die

BANTAM BOOKS

NEW YORK • TORONTO • LONDON • SYDNEY • AUCKLAND

RL 5, age 10 and up

PLEASE DON'T DIE
A Bantam Book / November 1993

The Starfire logo is a registered trademark of Bantam Books,
a division of Bantam Doubleday Dell Publishing Group, Inc.
Registered in U.S. Patent and Trademark Office and elsewhere.

ISBN 0-553-56262-2

Published simultaneously in the United States and Canada

Bantam Books are published by Bantam Books, a division of Bantam
Doubleday Dell Publishing Group, Inc. Its trademark, consisting of the
words "Bantam Books" and the portrayal of a rooster, is Registered in
U.S. Patent and Trademark Office and in other countries. Marca Regis-
trada. Bantam Books, 1540 Broadway, New York, New York 10036.

PRINTED IN THE UNITED STATES OF AMERICA

RAD   0 9 8 7 6 5 4 3 2

Please Don't Die

One

KATIE O'ROARK COULDN'T believe her eyes. She peered out the car window at the building of wood and glass and river rock that rose majestically out of the clearing in the North Carolina mountain woods. Her heart hammered in anticipation.

"Do you suppose that's it?" her father asked. "It's an impressive-looking place to spend the summer."

"More like a resort than a dorm for sick kids," her mother added.

They had almost missed the small sign on the highway marking the turnoff for Jenny House, and her father had driven onto the property and along the rustic road cautiously. Beside her in the backseat, Josh glowered at the building lined with decks that jutted out over the back of the mountain. "You can change your mind," he reminded her. "You don't have to stay the whole twelve weeks."

They had argued about it ever since the invitation had come in May. But a letter promising to reveal the identity of JWC—the mysterious benefactor who had given Katie the one hundred thousand dollars that had helped, in part, to pay for her very expensive heart transplant operation and anti-rejection drug maintenance program—had been an irresistible lure. "I have to meet JWC," Katie told Josh as her father parked the car. "And all my doctors approve of my coming. I'm fine now, Josh. Besides, you've got a job at the newspaper office. You'll see, the time will fly. I owe JWC a lot."

"The original letter said there were no strings attached to the money you got."

"This is a different kind of string, Josh. Like the one I owe you for donating your brother's heart. I can't explain it. It's something I have to do." She understood how hard it was for him to let her go for the summer. After all, it was his brother Aaron's heart that was beating in her chest. And ever since her transplant operation, she and Josh Martel had become inseparable. It wasn't easy for Katie either. She loved Josh. It would be tough to be apart from him all summer.

"You don't even know what you'll be doing here," Josh grumbled.

"According to the invitation, I'll be with a group of sick teenagers."

"But what if you get sick again? What if you have

another episode of rejection? When I think about the last time—"

Katie placed the tips of her fingers against his lips to silence him. This had been a running argument throughout the two-day drive from Michigan to Jenny House. "But I *made* it, Josh. I pulled through. I'm fine and I'm here. And I plan on staying."

Katie crossed the wooden deck and entered the building. Inside, the facility smelled as fresh and new as it looked. A vaulted, beamed ceiling soared upward, and polished dark oak floors gleamed in the light streaming through plate-glass windows. Sitting areas with colorful rugs and groupings of furniture gave the gigantic room a cozy living-room atmosphere. A wall of solid river stone flanked one wall, where a mammoth fireplace was centered. Over it stretched a mantel made of a two-foot-thick beam of solid oak.

Above the mantel hung a painting that made Katie stop short. She gazed up at a black-haired girl wearing a velvet gown of midnight blue. The girl's eyes were bright blue, her expression wistful, as if she knew some sad secret. She looked real enough to step down from the canvas.

"Wow," Josh said softly, coming alongside Katie. "Who's that?"

"Maybe I'd better keep an eye on you this summer if every pretty girl is going to cause that kind of a reaction," Katie teased. "But you're right. She *is* gorgeous." Josh's face turned as red as his hair.

Katie's parents were talking to a receptionist behind a brass-railed registration desk on the other side of the vast room. "Let me call our director," the receptionist said, picking up the phone, as Katie and Josh walked over.

Moments later, a man emerged from a corridor. He was tall, slim, and blond, and wore an impeccably tailored navy blue suit. Although he was near her father in age, Katie thought he was one of the most handsome men she'd ever seen.

"You're Katie O'Roark," the man said. A smile lit up his face and made his emerald eyes sparkle. "I'm Richard Holloway."

"From the Wish Foundation?" She recognized his name from the check she'd been given by JWC.

"Actually, it was my father who administered the bulk of the Foundation's funds," Richard explained. "He died a while back."

Remembering her manners, Katie made a round of introductions. "Why have I been invited?" she asked after Richard led them to one of the comfortable sofas. "Your letter only said I'd be with other kids my age and that I was a guest. So when can I meet JWC? Who *is* JWC anyway?"

"Everything will be explained tonight," Richard replied. "This is the first time Jenny House has opened its doors, and we've invited five other teens who, like yourself, have received Wish money and have lived. You're the first one here, but the others should be arriving all afternoon."

Richard's comment caused a chill in Katie. It was an admission that she was one of a fortunate few still alive. "Your letter said there would be *sick* kids coming."

"The other guests will be arriving tomorrow."

"How many?" Katie's dad asked. He was a newspaperman, a sports writer, but Katie saw his reporter's instincts taking over. Even though he'd tried for over a year to discover the identity of JWC, he'd been unsuccessful, and Katie was certain that he'd insisted on driving her to Jenny House as much to satisfy his own curiosity as to make certain his daughter would be safe for the summer.

"Thirty kids between the ages of twelve and sixteen from all over the country."

"That certainly doesn't seem like very many for a place this size," Katie's mother commented.

"It's our very first summer of operation," Richard explained. "We thought it best to start small and work our way into larger groups. Plus we want to maintain a homey atmosphere. One of the things that sets Jenny House apart from other facilities of its type is that we'll be open year-round with a full-time staff—both professional and medical. It's our hope that kids who visit will come back at any time they feel the need to get away. Jenny House is a place to rest, have fun, make new friends."

"So you're more than a summer camp?"

"Much more. We're not just for kids with specific diseases. Any sick teen is welcome on a doctor's recommendation. Plus it's free. It was the wish of the house's benefactor that no one ever need pay in order to stay."

"Then JWC isn't the person responsible for this place?" Katie asked. She was a little disappointed, wondering if she'd *ever* get information about the One Last Wish benefactor. She seemed no closer to knowing anything about JWC than she'd been at home in Ann Arbor.

"Jenny House is supported by an endowment from a widow, a former client of my father's. Sadly, she died right before this facility was completed. She left me in charge." Richard smiled and stood. "Why don't you get settled in, Katie? I'm being summoned to the phone."

At the desk, the receptionist was gesturing to him. He asked one of his assistants, Penny Carson, to show Katie and her family around the grounds.

They rode in a golf cart and saw riding stables, a lake with boats, tennis courts, a softball field, and a picnic area. Walking trails, leading through cool green woods and panoramic views of distant mountains, made Jenny House even more spectacular. Back in the main lodge, they visited a clinic, a gym, an indoor pool, a cafeteria, and a game room filled with video and table games. On each of the upper floors, there were spacious dormlike rooms and a central kitchen and living area, as well as a large rec room.

"This is where you'll be staying," Penny told Katie, leading her inside a sunny room decorated in green and white with hot pink accents. "You've been assigned three roommates. You'll learn more tonight at the special meeting, but right now you get first dibs on the beds."

Katie selected the one nearest the window and asked her dad and Josh to bring up her stuff. "This is sort of an experiment, isn't it?" Katie asked when she and Penny were alone.

"In a way, yes. But it's a very controlled one. Our staff includes two nurses, a psychologist, a gang of support workers—and of course, Mr. Holloway."

Penny added, "I'm the activities director, and I've spent over a month here getting ready for our grand opening. I've never seen anyone so determined to give sick and hurting kids a refuge as Mr. Holloway. I understand he left a successful law practice in order to take on this job. He's trying to fulfill someone's dream, but believe me, it's become his dream now. And after you've spent time around Jenny House . . . well, take it from me, it will become *your* dream also."

Later, in the parking lot, Katie said good-bye to her anxious parents. "It's a lovely place, but if you decide you don't like it, we'll come get you," her mother said.

"I'll be fine, Mom."

"And should you get sick—" her dad suggested.

"I won't get sick."

She hugged them both, took Josh by the hand, and walked with him into the woods. Under the canopy of the green trees, he took her in his arms and held her fiercely. "I don't want to leave you."

"I'll write."

"Me too. I love you, Katie," he whispered.

"I love you too." She rose on her toes and kissed

him, then together they walked back to the car. She watched her father drive away. Watched until the car disappeared on the winding road through the woods. Until Josh's face was only a speck in the back window and she stood alone next to Jenny House.

Two

By seven that night, three more girls and two guys had joined Katie at Jenny House. Each had also received One Last Wish money, one as long as five years before, and each had done something different with it. The group was medically diverse. Katie had been given a new heart, Ashley and Carol Ann had been victims of leukemia, Jeff was a hemophiliac, Todd was fighting aplastic anemia, and Stacey had kidney disease. None of them seemed to know why they had been selected by JWC, and no one had a clue as to their benefactor's identity.

They settled in front of the fireplace to get better acquainted. One of the staff had laid a fire, for although it was June, the evening mountain air was cool. Katie gazed into the dancing flames and thought of Josh. She missed him and wished he could be with her.

"I thought I'd pop from curiosity about JWC," Carol Ann confessed. "I can't tell you what that money meant to my family and me. I stashed some of it away for college and blew a chunk on the world's best shopping spree . . . in Paris!"

Ashley laughed. "I have two brothers, and I bought each of us new cars. Need I mention how good my brothers are to me now?"

"I treated my dad and me to the Super Bowl two years ago," Jeff declared. "The rest goes toward college. If I'm still around."

Katie listened with avid interest. Not only because it was fun to hear what others had done with their money, but because she felt a thread of connection with these strangers. She knew some of them were still fighting their battles with their illnesses. But she realized the thing they held most in common was an unquenchable desire to live. JWC had touched each of their lives and made a difference.

Katie was feeling at ease with the group when Richard Holloway joined them. He'd traded in his suit for casual slacks and a pale blue sweater. "I want you to feel perfectly at home while you're here, so if you have *any* problems or concerns, please bring them to me directly. Our medical personnel have talked to each of your doctors, and so we know how to deal with any medical situations, but the emotional"—he glanced at each of them—"well, that's part of the reason you're here. And part of the reason why other kids have been invited.

"It's our hope that you will become Big Brothers and Sisters to the ones coming in. All are sick and in need of friends." Richard paused. "Questions?"

"When can we meet JWC?" Carol Ann asked what was on all their minds.

"When you get to heaven," Richard said quietly.

Katie hadn't known what answer to expect, but this one was a total shock. "Are you saying JWC is dead?" she asked.

Richard stood, walked to the fireplace, and gazed up at the portrait of the young woman. "Her name was Jennifer Warren Crawford, and she was diagnosed with leukemia at age sixteen. That was back in 1978, before bone marrow transplants, before so many of the new drugs and treatments were available."

Katie's gaze shifted up toward the gilt-framed canvas. Again she was struck by the girl's ethereal beauty. *Sixteen.* That was how old she'd been when she'd received her new heart. And 1978. Why, that was years ago!

Richard turned to face the group. "Jenny was a unique person. She'd been born privileged. Her parents died when she was six, and she went to live with her paternal grandmother. The bond between the two of them was unshakable." He leaned against the oak mantel. "When she was first diagnosed, her grandmother spared no expense in seeking a cure for her. There was none. In the hospital, she made friends. I can't explain how those friendships made a difference in her brief life, but they did.

"Before she died, Jenny asked her grandmother to

help set up the One Last Wish Foundation. She wanted to give her money to people like herself— teenagers who were facing death." Richard began to pace in front of the fireplace while he talked. "You know, if you ask the average person on the street, 'What would you do if you had one hundred thousand dollars?' everyone has an answer.

"But if you ask, 'What would you do if you had one hundred thousand dollars *and* you were dying?' . . .well, the answer often changes. It's funny how the specter of death influences a person's choices."

Katie considered his words carefully. He was right. Last summer, when she thought she might die, she'd begged her parents to make sure her Wish money went to Josh for his future. The money had no value to her unless it could do something for somebody else. Suddenly, she understood Jennifer Crawford's mind-set perfectly. JWC's money had had no value to the beautiful young girl unless it could help others.

"So her grandmother set up the Wish Foundation?" Jeff asked.

"That's right."

"But why all the secrecy?" Ashley wanted to know. "And how did I get chosen?"

"The anonymity was Jenny's wish. The selection process was complicated, set up by Jenny's grandmother and my father, who administered the funds. Over the years, the Foundation has given away over five million dollars."

Katie heard herself gasp with the others. "Are we the only survivors?" she asked.

"Not at all. Remember, the Foundation's been giving away Wish money for close to fifteen years. Of
course, as medical science has improved, so have the
odds for living. I'd say that one in seven of the Foundation's recipients are still alive." For the first time,
Richard grinned, and Katie was struck by his warmth
and charm. She wanted to know what part he had
played in Jenny's life, but didn't have the nerve to
ask.

"You told me that this place"—Katie gestured
broadly—"was a widow's dying wish. Did you mean
Jenny's grandmother?"

"Yes. She wanted Jenny House to offer for you survivors all the things Jenny couldn't have during her
hospitalizations. She wanted it to be a refuge, a place
for friends to meet, a 'safe' place where you could
take time out from the realities of illness. Jenny
House can't make problems go away, but it can offer
a brief escape."

Katie thought the mission sounded idealistic and
lofty, and she certainly found it appealing. It would
be good to be with others who'd been at death's
door, who truly understood the unique perspective
she'd experienced. Even as close as she felt to Josh,
even though he'd endured the death of his only
brother, he could never grasp what her brush with
death had been like for her. And despite all the
medications she was taking to keep her body from
rejecting her new heart, there were no guarantees. If
there was some way for her to reach out to the kids
like herself . . .

"We have a state-of-the-art game room," Richard

said, interrupting her thoughts and changing the course of the discussion. "Refreshments too. The rest of the staff is down there waiting to meet you. Maybe you'd like to go down with me and give it a try. After all, one of the main reasons you're here is to have fun."

Katie had plenty of questions, but she realized there would be time to ask them in the weeks ahead. It seemed her only obligation for the summer was to have a good time and to be a friend. She figured she could manage both.

Katie lagged behind the others as they started downstairs, pausing to glance back at the crackling fire, the stone wall, and the portrait of Jennifer Crawford. The girl's mysterious smile beckoned. Jenny had signed her Wish letter, *Your Forever Friend*. Odd to call someone "friend" whom she'd never met. Yet Jenny had acted as *her* friend. Jenny Crawford had reached through time with her gift, and touched her life. She'd made it matter.

The next morning, Katie was up early, anticipating meeting the other girls assigned to her room. The night before, after meeting the staff, she'd played several games of laser tag, and as a natural athlete, she'd quickly scored high points. Yet it was the VR—virtual reality—games that had fascinated her the most.

She'd put on a special helmet, and suddenly, she'd found herself in a three-dimensional world, full of lifelike images and stereo sound, taking a kayak ride through white-water rapids. It had seemed so real, she'd felt the rushing waters and smelled the icy foam. Her heart had pounded, and adrenaline had flowed through her as if she were poised to start a big track event.

"Awesome," she'd declared, handing over the helmet to Jeff, who chose to fight off a fire-breathing dragon with a laser-sword.

In the morning sunlight, Katie put the fun of the previous night behind her and prepared for her incoming roommates. Sitting cross-legged on her bed, she scanned a paper revealing basic facts about them.

Amanda Burdick was thirteen, the youngest, and a leukemia victim in her second remission. Lacey Duval was sixteen and a diabetic. Katie didn't know much about diabetes, but had never thought it life-threatening.

The last girl on her list was a fourteen-year-old named Chelsea James. Katie's breath caught when she read that Chelsea was a lifelong victim of a congenital heart defect that had slowly worsened over the years. No surgery could help. In fact, Chelsea's only hope for long-term survival would be a heart transplant! Katie's sympathies went out to Chelsea immediately. Katie knew how it felt; after all, she had survived what Chelsea had yet to endure. She honestly believed she could offer encouragement to this girl. She looked forward to meeting her.

It was noon when Amanda arrived. She was a tiny, pixielike girl with big brown eyes that dominated her face. Her hair was a sleek cap, but once her parents left, Amanda tugged off the hair and tossed it casually onto the bed.

"A wig," she explained with an impish smile at the

expression on Katie's face. "The darn thing's hot, and I hate it."

Katie grinned, liking Amanda instantly. Amanda's own hair was nothing but tufts on her bald head, yet it was obvious she wasn't self-conscious about it. "Go for comfort," Katie urged.

Just then, a blond girl wearing a knockout fashion ensemble swept into the room. She eyed them haughtily and announced, "I'm Lacey. But don't bother being friendly. I'm not staying. Just as soon as I can figure out a way to blow this place, I'm out of here!"

Three

"WHERE'RE YOUR PARENTS?" Katie asked, unsure of how to respond to Lacey's announcement.

"I left them standing downstairs, arguing. Honestly, what a pain! They argued on the plane all the way from Miami. Dad rented a car at the airport, and they fought the whole way out here. I got tired of listening to them." Lacey paced to the window and peered out.

Amanda asked, "So if you hate their arguing, why do you want to leave?"

"I don't want to be around them, but I sure don't want to be stuck in this place either. I wouldn't have ever come on my own. It was my doctor's idea. He's also my uncle, and he decided this would be a good place for me to spend the summer. He talked my parents into bringing me. Although they sure didn't need much persuading."

Katie figured it was her job to encourage Lacey to stay. "It's a really neat place. You should give it a chance."

"Who wants to hang around a bunch of sick people?" Lacey said, turning from the window and crossing her arms. "I don't even attend diabetic camp for a week. Why should I want to be stuck here for a whole summer?"

Just then, one of the staff entered, carrying a set of matched luggage. "Are these yours?" he asked.

Lacey practically ignored him. "I'm *not* staying," she insisted.

"Where should I put them?"

Before Lacey could make a suggestion, Katie intervened. "Why not take the bed next to mine? Amanda won't mind, will you?" She gave Amanda a pleading look.

"I wanted this bed anyway," Amanda replied cheerfully, crossing to one of the beds on the other side of the room. Katie could have kissed her.

The man heaved the suitcases onto the bed. "Your folks are talking to Mr. Holloway, the director. You want to come tell them good-bye?"

Lacey tossed her long blond hair, and Katie thought she saw tears glistening in the girl's eyes. "Tell them good-bye for me. That is, if they stop going for each other's throat long enough to hear you."

Although Lacey was acting disagreeable, Katie felt pity for her. It was hard enough coping with health problems without having to deal with warring parents too. Her own parents' arguments had always centered on her stubborn insistence to run track after her transplant, but she'd never doubted that they cared deeply for one another. "Look," Katie said, "I know this isn't much fun for you, but in a way we're all in the same boat. I had plenty of other things I could have been doing this summer. I left a terrific boyfriend back in Ann Arbor. How about you? Do you have a guy?"

Lacey swiped at her eyes and sat on the bed. "No one special."

Amanda spoke up. "I'd love to have a boyfriend, but all I've done for the past year is go in and out of the hospital. Not a cool place to meet guys."

"You never know," Katie replied. "That's where I met mine."

"In the hospital? How? Is he sick too?" Amanda flooded her with questions.

Katie couldn't help smiling. "It's a long story." She wished Lacey were as agreeable and pleasant as Amanda. She shot Lacey a sideward glance to check her interest level. Lacey was plucking at the bedspread and ignoring them. "And it's a great story too. I'll be glad to tell you later. Maybe once our other roommate arrives. Why don't you unpack—put your stuff away."

Amanda set right to work. Lacey maintained her sullen expression. Still, she eventually began to open her suitcases and put away her things. Katie had never seen such an array of cosmetics, hair gear, and perfume bottles as Lacey put out on one of the dressers.

"Do you use all that stuff?" Amanda asked, her large, expressive eyes wide with curiosity.

"All the girls at my school use makeup. It's cool."

"My mom won't allow me to wear makeup yet. She says I have to wait until ninth grade—which is like *forever*!"

Katie hoped Lacey had the good sense not to comment on Amanda's lack of sophistication. Lacey crowded the bottles closer together. "I've been wearing makeup since I was eleven."

"But you're so pretty," Amanda declared. "Why do you need so much?"

Lacey was noticeably taken aback by Amanda's comment, and Katie figured that the small, dark-eyed girl could charm the skin off a snake and never know it.

"I wonder where our other roomie is," Katie interjected, diverting both girls' attention.

"If she's smart, she stayed home," Lacey muttered.

A rap on the door made them turn. A brown-haired woman peered anxiously through the doorway. "Is there a Katie O'Roark here?"

"That's me." Katie stepped forward.

"They told me downstairs that you were in charge."

"Well, I'm sort of supervising. But I'm not really a boss or anything."

"I'm Chelsea's mother." The woman came into the room, followed by a man carrying a frail, sickly girl.

"I can walk, Dad," Chelsea kept repeating, obviously embarrassed.

"No use expending too much energy," her father

said. He placed her on the one empty bed as if she were a fragile piece of glass. Katie did think Chelsea looked delicate enough to break. Her lips held a slightly bluish cast that made Katie's stomach constrict. She knew what it was like to have a bad heart and struggle for every breath of air.

"Are you all right, honey?" Chelsea's mother felt Chelsea's forehead, then clung to her hand.

"I'm fine," Chelsea mumbled. She cast the other girls an apologetic glance, then looked again at her mother. "Dr. Hooper told you it was all right for me to come. I'll be all right."

Chelsea's mother wrung her hands together. "I just hate leaving you. A summer is such a long time for you to stay away."

"I agree," Lacey said indifferently.

Katie felt like slugging her. "I know why they put Chelsea in my room," Katie offered. "You see, I had a heart condition once too. So, I'll know how to look out for her."

"That's what we've been told," Chelsea's father said, but her mother failed to look relieved. He took his wife's elbow. "Come on, Lorraine. This prolonged good-bye isn't healthy." He stooped and kissed his daughter's cheek. "You're going to do fine. And we can be here in a matter of hours if you need us."

A staff worker entered and deposited Chelsea's luggage. "I need to help her put her things away," her mother said. "I don't want her straining herself."

"I can do it, Mother," Chelsea insisted, scooting off the bed and hauling her suitcase off the floor.

"Don't do that!" Her mother hurried to help her lift the piece of luggage.

It took several more minutes before Chelsea could get her parents out of the room, but once they were gone, she turned toward the others and said, "Sorry about that."

"What's their problem?" Lacey asked. "Haven't you ever been away from home before?"

"No," Chelsea replied. The look on her face was sincere. "But don't worry. I'm not as helpless as they want me to be. I've got a lousy heart, but I can still manage. I promise not to be a drag."

Katie was reminded of how freaked out her parents had been when her heart disease had incapacitated her. She'd hated the way her mother had hovered over her and made her feel like an invalid, so she understood Chelsea's frustration completely. "We've all got parent problems," Katie said, giving Lacey a sidelong glance. "It goes with the territory. But we're all looking forward to having a fun summer."

Lacey snorted, and Katie shot her a warning look. Amanda stepped up to the foot of Chelsea's bed. "I can't wait to go exploring. Will you be able to go with us?"

"If I pace myself. I just have to be careful not to exert myself too much."

"No problem of *that*," Lacey said. "This place is nothing but a big Back to Nature experience."

"What's wrong with that?"

Lacey rolled her eyes. "I'm used to parties and fast

cars. The crowd I run with would go nuts with all these trees and squirrels."

Amanda giggled. "You made a joke. Trees . . . squirrels . . . nuts . . . That's funny."

Lacey didn't look amused, but Katie was once again taken by the younger girl's quick mind and cheerful disposition. "Listen, Lacey, we're all in this together. Why not make the best of it?"

"I told you, I'm not used to hanging around with sick people. I'm not sick!"

Katie wished she knew more about diabetes. "I'm not either," she said levelly. "So all the more reason for us to have a good time."

"You're not the boss around here."

"I said I wasn't." Katie could feel her temper rising. "But I plan to spend the summer here, and I plan on having fun." She glanced from Amanda to Chelsea.

"Me too," they said in unison.

Katie shrugged. "Majority rules. We're all going to have fun."

Lacey made an exasperated grunt and marched into the bathroom. She slammed the door behind her. "Is it something I said?" Katie asked innocently. Chelsea and Amanda laughed, and Katie added, "Look, she's just having a hard time adjusting. Let's give her plenty of space. She'll come around."

Katie wasn't at all sure Lacey would and wondered if she could endure a whole summer with someone like Lacey. Then she watched Chelsea shuffle over to a dresser, her arms full of clothes. She realized that every breath the girl took was an effort. How could she abandon someone who was trying as hard as Chelsea? Or someone as sweet as Amanda?

What have I gotten myself into? she wondered. How could she possibly make a difference in any of these girls' lives?

Four

Dear Josh,

I know it's only been twenty-four hours since I last wrote, but I just want you to know that I miss you and think about you all the time.

Not much has changed since my last letter. I've been here four days, but it seems longer. Lacey is still being a pain. Amanda is all sweetness and light and so adorable, I'd like to take her home with me. You know how I've always wished I had a sister. But with my luck, I'd probably get one like Lacey. (Sorry —that isn't nice.)

It's poor Chelsea I worry about the most. She never complains, but I know she's scared stiff. She's told me that this is the first time she's ever been away

*from home. Can you imagine? But she's had her
bum heart ever since birth, and it's not getting any
better. She's never even attended regular school.
She's been tutored and home-schooled all her life.
She's always got her nose in a book. She's says it's
the only form of escape that her heart can take. (The
black humor around this place is crazy).*

*The staff is fantastic. Mr. Holloway is always
around, asking if we're having a good time. There's
a trail ride and a picnic planned for tomorrow. The
horses are supposed to be tame, but Chelsea is ner-
vous. She really wants to go, but she's afraid her
heart might act up. Seeing her brings back my own
experience. I never want to go through that again.
So, I never forget to take my medications.*

*Which reminds me—Lacey has to be reminded every
day, morning and evening, to take her insulin shots.
She truly hates them, but without them, she'll get
very sick. Hospital sick. You'd think that would
make her afraid of not taking her shots, but it
doesn't.*

*Well, I don't want this letter to sound whiny (which
it does), so I'd better close. Write soon. I love you a
bunch.*

Katie

*P.S. Did I mention that I miss you? Say hi to
Gramps for me.*

"Are you writing to your boyfriend?" Amanda asked, coming up alongside Katie's bed. She was dressed in a pink nightshirt that pictured a cuddly lop-eared rabbit on the front.

"Sure am."

Amanda picked up the framed photo of Josh on the bedside table Katie shared with Lacey. "He's so cute," Amanda said. "Tell me how you met him."

Katie saw that Chelsea had put down her book to listen. Lacey was doing her nails and pointedly ignoring the other girls. "I got his brother's heart," Katie began dramatically. Amanda's eyes widened, and Chelsea closed her book and came over to Katie's bed and sat down. Even Lacey appeared to be listening.

Katie went on to tell how Aaron had died on the football field of a brain hemorrhage, and how Josh and his grandfather had agreed to donate Aaron's organs for transplantation. She described how Josh figured out who'd received his brother's heart by reading a newspaper column Katie's dad had written, and how Josh had begun to haunt the hospital in an effort to see her and to connect with his brother. "Josh was really grieving," Katie explained. "But even though he knew Aaron was dead, he wanted to be with him. Somehow, knowing Aaron's heart was beating inside me made him still alive.

"Anyway, once I met Josh, once I knew about his brother, I wanted him near me. I was so grateful for the organ donation, but after a while, I became grateful for Josh. He's one in a million."

Amanda's brown eyes had filled with tears. "That's

so romantic. Really wonderful, don't you think so?" She turned toward Chelsea and Lacey. The blond Lacey shrugged, pretending indifference, but Katie could tell that the story had hooked her.

Chelsea asked, "Doesn't it feel weird knowing someone else's heart is beating inside you?"

Katie understood the girl's interest, since she was facing a transplant in her future. "The transplant center has a support program—you know, shrinks to help you deal with such things. But of course, it bothered me. I don't think about it at all anymore. Aaron's heart is keeping me alive. I have Josh. I can run track again."

"You run?" Chelsea looked surprised.

"I won a big race at the Transplant Olympics. Josh helped me train; he's a runner too. And I'm on the track team at my high school."

"I've never been able to run. I've always wanted to be able to run against the wind and feel it in my hair."

"You've never *run?*" Lacey asked. "Not even when you were a kid?"

"I couldn't." Chelsea gazed down self-consciously. "I've never been able to do any kind of strenuous activity. My heart can't take it. If I try, I pass out, and sometimes I end up in the hospital. I hate being stuck in the hospital."

The room fell silent. Finally, Katie said, "My transplant gave me back my life. I can't imagine not running track."

"Are you the star of your team?" Amanda asked.

Katie laughed, which relieved the somber mood in

the room. "Hardly. You see, I missed most of my junior year because of my transplant. So did Josh, because he hung around with me so much. Anyway, we both repeated eleventh grade, and so we'll be seniors in September. I didn't get to graduate with my class this June, but I do get another shot at the women's state track title next year, because I still have a year of eligibility."

"You had to stay behind when all your friends graduated?" Amanda asked. "I wouldn't like doing that."

Katie thought of Melody, her best friend, who would be a freshman at Boston College in September. "Sure, staying back a grade is hard for me. But I'll keep in touch with them, and I didn't stay behind because I flunked. I just missed too many days of school to be advanced."

"It took you a year to recover from your transplant?" Chelsea asked, a frown on her thin face.

Katie decided against telling her about the episode of rejection that almost took her life and the long recuperation period that had followed. "Oh, it takes a while to get back on your feet," she said simply. "But I'll always be glad I got a new heart. It was worth all the hospital time, all the discomfort. I mean, look at me now."

"I hated missing school when I was in the hospital," Amanda offered. "I got diagnosed with leukemia when I was in third grade and relapsed in fifth. I just got out of the hospital a few months ago because of complications, but at least I finished seventh grade with my class." She grinned. "Partly because my dad works for a TV station, and he arranged to have a camera set up in my classrooms so I could attend classes even though I was home in bed. I couldn't stand it if all my friends got passed and I had to stay behind."

"What about you, Lacey? Has your diabetes messed up your school life any?" Katie asked.

Lacey tightened the lid on her bottle of fingernail polish and scooted off her bed. "Just because I have to take insulin doesn't make me sick. I don't have any health problems. I never miss school. In fact, none of my friends even know about my diabetes. Now, if you'll excuse me, I'm going to brush my teeth."

With that, she flounced into the bathroom and shut the door firmly behind her. Katie stared after her, feeling put down and shut out from anything to do with Lacey Duval.

Katie woke with a start. The room was dark, and she saw no trace of dawn through the partially drawn window shade. As she wondered what had disturbed her, her gaze was drawn to a hairline crack of light coming from beneath the bathroom door. She heard muffled sounds from inside and was instantly awake.

Her first concern was for Chelsea. Had all the talk about a heart transplant upset the younger girl? But when she peered across the room at Chelsea's bed, she saw that Chelsea was still sound asleep. In the bed next to Chelsea's, Amanda also slept soundly. That left only one person.

Katie eased out of bed and tiptoed to the bathroom. She pressed her ear to the door and heard Lacey fumbling around. Katie rapped lightly. "Are you all right?"

"Go away." Lacey's voice sounded quivery.

"I'm coming in," Katie said. She pushed open the door and found Lacey sitting on the floor, breathing erratically. Her face was the color of paste, and she was trembling. "What's wrong?" Quickly, Katie crouched beside her. "I'll call for some help."

"No!" Lacey's tone was sharp. "I'm having . . . a . . . reaction. Open this."

Katie took a small foil packet marked "Instant Glucose" from Lacey's shaky hand. She tore it open, removed two flat round tablets, and watched Lacey shove them into her mouth, then flop weakly back against the outside of the tub.

Anxiously, Katie waited. In a minute, color began to return to Lacey's face, and her breathing grew slower and more regular. Finally, Lacey mumbled, "It's over."

By now Katie was trembling. "What's over? What happened?"

"I told you, I had an insulin reaction." Lacey struggled to her feet. Katie tried to help, but Lacey pushed her away. "It's just something diabetics have to learn to live with," Lacey said. She bent over the sink and splashed cold water on her face. "Your blood sugar gets too low, and you need to eat something sweet to get it back up. Now I'll eat some crackers so it won't happen again. I'm telling you, I'm okay."

In fact, she did look perfectly fine. "You should have told me," Katie said. "I could have helped you.

Someone should know how to help you when you get sick."

"I can help myself," Lacey replied. "I would have been fine."

Katie wanted to argue with her that she *hadn't* been doing fine, but she didn't want to risk waking the others with an argument. "Whatever you say." Katie returned to her bed and jerked the covers up to her chin.

Minutes later, she heard Lacey slide into the bed next to hers. Katie lay silently in the dark, seething, when Lacey's voice floated to her in a soft whisper. "Uh—thanks," Lacey said.

"You're welcome," Katie answered curtly. Then she turned herself away from Lacey and toward the wall.

Five

THE RIDING TRAIL wound through woods of sunlight-dappled leaves and patches of vibrantly colored wildflowers. Katie breathed in the cool summer morning air and squeezed her knees against her horse's flanks, making him accelerate his plodding pace. She drew alongside Chelsea, whose big chestnut mount appeared to be half dozing along the leaf-littered trail. "How're you doing?" she asked.

"Super." Chelsea gave a contented grin. "If my horse can stay awake."

"He does look comfortable."

"And to think I was scared he'd take off running with me in the saddle."

Both girls laughed, and Chelsea's horse pricked up his ears. "Careful," Katie warned. "Let's not wake him."

Ahead of them on the trail, Katie watched the swaying rounded rump of Amanda's horse. The girl was chattering away at Jeff McKensie, the seventeen-year-old from Colorado who was a hemophiliac. Of all the kids who'd received Wish money, Katie liked Jeff best. She'd met him down at the indoor pool doing laps on their first morning at Jenny House. "One of the few safe exercises for a bleeder," Jeff had explained. "Contact sports are too dangerous. We could bleed to death if we're hit too hard."

Jeff was blond, tall, and slim, with eyes that changed from blue to gray according to what he was wearing. Katie swam laps with him and grew fond of him, talking freely about track and running and Josh. "My girl and I broke up right before I came," Jeff told her that first morning.

"I'm sorry."

"Me too. I understand, though. Hooking up with a bleeder doesn't make for a good long-term relationship, if you know what I mean. Hemophiliacs are always at risk. If not from injury, then from blood transfusions contaminated with hepatitis or worse."

Watching Jeff and Amanda on the trail ahead of her gave Katie pause. Looking at them, no one would ever suspect that they both carried deadly disorders inside their bodies. "Looks like our little Amanda is having a good time," Katie heard Chelsea say.

"Jeff's a nice guy."

"I hope our little romantic roomie doesn't get any ideas," Chelsea commented.

"Ideas?"

"Look at the way she's looking at him. If he were

an ice-cream cone . . ." Chelsea let the sentence trail.

"You're right," Katie agreed. "How did I miss it?"

"I'm a trained observer. I've spent my whole life on the outside looking in. I've gotten pretty good at reading people."

Katie felt sorry for Chelsea. Her bad heart had truly kept her out of life's mainstream, and considering how her parents all but suffocated her, it was no wonder. "How about you, Chelsea? Have you ever liked one special guy?"

"Where would I meet one?"

Chelsea's eyes met Katie's, and the depth of sadness and longing in them made a lump rise in Katie's throat. "You'll find someone special someday," she said. "You're only fourteen."

"I'll be fifteen soon."

"You will? When? We should have a birthday party."

"But Lacey can't eat birthday cake."

"I have a feeling Lacey does pretty much whatever she wants to do."

"She's not as tough as she pretends to be." Chelsea shifted in the saddle, and her horse snorted, as if protesting the movement.

Katie shook her head. "I'm not so sure."

"I am. Us people watchers can't be fooled. She was hanging on every word of your story about you and Josh. I have a feeling Lacey just wants to be liked."

"She has an odd way of showing it. She could be nicer." Even as she spoke, Katie felt a pang of guilt. She shouldn't be voicing her opinion of Lacey to

Chelsea. Especially since she was supposed to be a role model.

The line of horses drew to a halt.

"What's up?" Chelsea asked.

Katie craned her neck. "Looks like a large clearing ahead. I guess that's where we're having our picnic." The line began to move again, and soon Katie had passed from the cool interior of the woods into an enormous sun-drenched meadow. Tall grass brushed the bellies of the horses. At the far end of the field there was a concrete shelter with tables and benches. The aroma of barbecue drifted on the summer breeze.

She heard Jeff shout, "Let's go!" and saw him dig his heels into the sides of his horse. The animal broke into a gallop toward the shelter. Soon, many of the group had urged their horses into a run through the field.

Katie wanted to race her horse too, but the look of fright on Chelsea's face stopped her. "I'm sticking with you," Katie said. "There's no hurry."

Chelsea flashed her a grateful smile. "I . . . um . . . I've just never ridden before. I don't want to do something dumb—like fall off and spoil the picnic for everybody."

By the time Katie and Chelsea had plodded up to the shelter, the other horses had been tied and were grazing off to one side. Kids lounged around the tables, sipping sodas and talking. Several members of the staff were manning the barbecue pit and asking for hamburger orders. Once Katie and Chelsea had dismounted and tied their horses with the others, they headed toward the shelter.

Amanda jogged up, her brown eyes sparkling. "I'm having such a great time. Did you see me riding with Jeff? He talked to me the whole time. Can you believe it? Only me."

Katie could see how Jeff's attention had affected the petite girl, and she didn't want to throw cold water on her enthusiasm, but Jeff was four years older than Amanda. "Jeff's a nice guy," Katie said.

"He told me that you and he are friends." She grabbed Katie's hand and tugged impatiently. "Can we go for a little walk?"

"Don't mind me," Chelsea told them. "I'm going to get a cola and sit down."

Impatiently, Amanda dragged Katie back toward the line of grazing horses. "So what do you think?" She dropped Katie's hand and peered up at her.

"What do I think about what?"

"About me and Jeff." Momentarily at a loss for words, Katie stooped and pulled up a pale yellow flower. "I mean, he's your friend. Do you think he could like someone like me?" Amanda prodded.

"Golly, Amanda, I don't know . . ."

"I've never had a real boyfriend, you know. My other friends have. But I've always been recovering from chemo—which isn't exactly a turn-on for guys."

"Gee, I didn't even notice guys were alive for years," Katie said. "But then, I was a late bloomer," she added when she saw Amanda's crestfallen expression. "Is it really so important to you to have a boyfriend?"

"Look at me. I'm almost fourteen and I look ten. It's because of the chemo, you know."

"No, I didn't realize—"

"It's stunted my growth. I'll never catch up to my friends. Everybody's wearing bras, and I'm flat as a pancake."

"Everybody? Even the guys?"

Amanda offered a sheepish smile. "You know what I mean. I hate being a shrimp. When I put on lipstick, I look like a little girl trying to play dress-up. And it's all because of my cancer."

Katie felt a wave of pity. Inside Amanda's childlike body was an almost-woman struggling to break free. Katie's body had developed and changed, and she'd simply accepted it. In some ways, she'd resented it. The changes had slowed her ability to race, and soon she'd been unable to beat boys on the playground as she'd done for years. "I didn't know chemo affected kids that way."

"Well, it does. There're lots of side effects. You get so sick, you can't stand up. Your hair falls out. You get sores all over—you look really gross. It's pretty nasty stuff. But that's the way it has to be, because without it, you'd die in record time. I hate having cancer."

Katie hadn't heard the usually cheerful, upbeat Amanda sound so upset before. "I guess we've all wondered, 'Why me?'" Katie said. "I sure did when my heart started giving out."

Amanda gazed off toward distant mountains shrouded in blue haze. "I guess you must think I'm a real whiner."

"Not at all. Even though my problem was different, I felt the same way. Without a new heart, I'd die. But I could only get a new heart if somebody else died. It was a heavy thought."

"So maybe you can see why I'd like a boyfriend. After two relapses, I may be running out of time."

The thought hit Katie like cold water. "But you're fine now."

"I was fine before I relapsed." Amanda turned back toward the shelter. "I'm sorry I started talking about this stuff. I really want to have a good time today. I'd really like to go find Jeff and see if he'll talk to me some more."

"There are other guys here closer to your age."

"So what? None of them is as hunky as Jeff."

"Good luck," Katie called as Amanda trotted off. Suddenly, she felt at loose ends, as if a dark cloud had scudded over the sun. Yet, when she looked around, the day was still beautiful, and the sounds of people having a good time floated through the clean, fresh air.

"You alone?" Jeff stepped from around the line of horses.

Startled, Katie wondered if he'd heard any of her conversation with Amanda. She fervently hoped not. Amanda would be embarrassed to tears if he had. "Are you?" she countered.

"I've got something to ask you." He stepped closer, glancing in all directions. "And a favor."

"What is it?"

"Put in a good word for me with Lacey Duval. I think she's something else."

Six

$\mathcal{C}\!\!\!\!\!\sim\!\!\!\!\mathcal{D}$

"LACEY? YOU'RE INTERESTED in Lacey? But I saw you with Amanda."

"Amanda's just a kid. Lacey's great-looking, and I've always had a weakness for blondes." Jeff grinned. "What's wrong with liking Lacey?"

"Nothing's wrong with it," Katie replied, feeling as if everything was wrong with it. She simply didn't want it to be true. Hadn't she just spent thirty minutes hearing Amanda pour her heart out about her hopes for her and Jeff? "Why don't you just go after Lacey yourself? Why involve me?"

"I have two sisters. I know how you girls stick together, and that one good word from a friend can go a long way toward opening a girl's eyes to some guy who's interested in her."

Katie almost asked, *"What makes you think Lacey's*

my friend?" but she thought better of it. Instead, she tried a different tack. "Lacey kind of keeps to herself. She didn't even want to come here this summer, but her doctor insisted. Maybe she's not the girl for you. Have you looked around? There're other girls. Maybe you can give another girl a try."

He shook his head. "No other girl appeals to me like Lacey. Face it, this place is ideal for someone like me. Health problems don't exactly attract the babes in the real world." He motioned toward the picnic tables, where almost everyone was seated eating burgers and hot dogs. "Not much competition either. Most of the guys are a lot younger."

"Just because your girlfriend back home broke up with you—"

"It took forever just to get her to date me," Jeff said soberly. "And our big romance lasted until I had a bleeding episode and ended up in the hospital. She dumped me real quick."

"She didn't have much character," Katie insisted, taking personally the sting of his former girlfriend's rejection.

"Rejection is a way of life when you're different— when you've got problems other kids don't understand. Your experience with Josh is one in a million. So, will you help me with Lacey?"

"Let me get this straight. You figure that since there's not much choice out here, then Lacey may find you appealing. That you're better than boredom?"

"That's why I like you, Katie. You catch on real fast. Look around." Jeff gestured toward the backdrop of misty blue mountains. "Can you think of a better place to keep a girl's undivided attention? Lots of scenery. Nothing to do but play. No distractions. Lacey has nothing to do but pay attention to me."

"I'm not sure that will matter one bit to Lacey. She's kind of determined to keep to herself."

"I love a challenge."

Jeff was refusing to be put off, which distressed Katie. How could she divert his attention from Lacey and direct it toward Amanda? "I still think you should go after her without my help."

"Are you telling me you won't help?"

Katie felt torn. She liked Jeff and Amanda both, and didn't want to see either of them hurt. Yet, how could she help the one without sabotaging the other? "Why don't you try it on your own? If I have to get involved, then maybe I will."

Jeff looked disappointed. "I was hoping you'd put in a good word for me."

Katie chewed on her bottom lip. "If I talk Lacey into it, how will you know if it's you she likes? Dating somebody shouldn't be as a favor to someone else."

"I can live with it."

Katie slugged his arm playfully. "Oh, you! Come on, give yourself a chance. Go for it on your own."

Jeff studied her thoughtfully, then put his arm around her shoulders. "All right. I won't put you on the spot. You're a good buddy. And the only one willing to do laps in the pool with me at six every morning. I'll see what kind of progress I can make on my own with Lacey."

Katie walked with him back to the picnic tables, feeling relieved. She figured she'd gotten out of Jeff's request without betraying Amanda's confidence. She only wished Jeff would forget about Lacey and give Amanda half a chance.

Later in the afternoon, they chose up sides for softball. Katie was captain of one team, and Jeff the other. She selected Lacey first, mostly to keep her off Jeff's team. Jeff chose Amanda, and the younger girl fairly glowed as she trotted over to his side.

By the time the game was over, Katie wished she'd been less charitable. Lacey couldn't hit the side of a barn, and Amanda had slugged in three home runs. "We trounced you guys," Amanda crowed as they rode back to the stables at Jenny House in the twilight.

"Don't rub it in," Katie said. "I've always been a poor loser."

Amanda leaned closer to Katie and whispered, "Jeff picked me for his team. That must mean something. What do you think, Katie? Do you think I have a chance with him?"

Amanda sounded so thrilled that Katie didn't even try to burst the younger girl's bubble about her hopeless crush. Up ahead, she saw Jeff rein in his horse beside Lacey's and hoped that the lengthening shadows in the woods would hide the sight from Amanda.

Why couldn't life be simple? she wondered. Why were people always drawn to what they couldn't have? She sighed, deciding that the problem was as old as time, and would never have an answer. At least, none she could come up with.

Dear Katie,

This is the longest summer of my life. I know it's only been three weeks since I left you at Jenny House, but even with my job, time drags. Your dad's helped me plenty, and I've already worked my way out of my mailroom duties. I went out with one of the reporters on his rounds (he covers the police beat), and that was fun. I don't think I'd like being a reporter, but being a cop seems interesting.

Sounds like you have your hands full with those roommates. I can't answer your question as to why a guy ignores a girl who's nuts about him to go after one who isn't. Maybe Jeff's just a slow learner. He's not coming on to you, is he? I mean, I can't figure how any guy could appreciate any other girl when you're around. (If this guy makes any moves on you, I'll come there personally and deal with him. Make sure he keeps his hands off YOU.)

Gramps has been doing little projects around the house. It takes him longer than it used to, but he gets the job done. He goes out to the cemetery every weekend to put fresh flowers on Gram's and Aaron's graves. He begged me to go with him. I did, but I really hated it. Not so much seeing Gram's grave. I mean, she was pretty old when she died. But it tears me up to see Aaron's. I still miss him, and I guess I always will. Then I remember that without his heart, there'd be no Katie in my life. And I can't imagine that either. I don't like thinking about it, so I'm not going back out there again.

I guess that's pretty much it from here. Try not to get too involved with Jeff and Lacey and Amanda. After this summer, you'll all go your separate ways. I really miss you, Katie, and I wish it was August already.

Love,

Josh

Katie ran her fingertips over Josh's distinctive signature when she finished reading his letter. She *did* miss him. Of course, his suggestion that Jeff might be interested in her was ludicrous. It had been a week since the picnic, and all Jeff talked about was Lacey. And all Amanda talked about was Jeff—privately and only to Katie. Lacey didn't say much of anything, but she did seem less belligerent. And she was taking her insulin shots on time.

Katie had grown sensitive to Lacey's moods. She saw a marked disintegration in Lacey's disposition whenever her blood sugar level dipped. And although Lacey didn't have another insulin reaction, Katie did notice that she would discreetly drink some orange juice or nibble on a candy bar at different times in the day.

Katie tucked Josh's letter in her drawer with the others from him and spied her calendar. She'd marked June 30 with a big red star, and the moment Chelsea ducked into the bathroom for a shower, Katie grabbed Lacey and Amanda. "Chelsea's birthday's coming up," she told them in a conspiratorial whisper. "Let's throw her a party. One terrific party that she'll never forget."

"That's a super idea!" Amanda bubbled with enthusiasm over Katie's suggestion.

"What about you, Lacey? You want to help?" Katie asked.

Lacey shrugged. "I guess so. What have you got in mind?"

"I'd like to invite everybody at Jenny House. We could hold it down in the lodge and the game room. I'm sure if I ask Mr. Holloway, he'll get us a cake."

"We've got to do more than eat cake and hang out in the game room. What kind of a dumb party is that?"

"And I suppose you're the party queen of Miami," Katie shot back, none too kindly.

Lacey gave her a bored look. "I've thrown my share of parties. Even had a couple raided by the cops."

"No lie?" Amanda's eyes grew round as saucers.

"I don't think that's the kind of party I had in mind," Katie said.

"No problem," Lacey replied. "We're so far out in the boondocks, the cops couldn't find this place."

Katie swallowed a retort. Why did Lacey continue to be negative about Jenny House? "So what great ideas do you have to make Chelsea's fifteenth birthday memorable?"

"I think a western theme would work. We could have a hayride and dancing and maybe a little carnival down in the rec room—you know, simple games like knocking over milk cartons and dropping clothespins into bottles for little prizes."

"And balloons," Amanda inserted. "And a big banner that says 'Happy Birthday' stretching across the fireplace."

"And everyone will have to bring some corny gag gift."

Katie had to admit that Lacey's ideas were good ones. "How can we keep it a surprise from Chelsea?"

"She takes a long nap every afternoon. We can make the decorations during the week and put everything up on the afternoon of her birthday."

"Maybe we can get a live band," Amanda suggested. "With fiddles and banjos."

"I'll talk to Mr. Holloway," Katie said. She liked Lacey's plans, and Lacey did sound as if she knew what she was doing. Plus her usual look of boredom had left her face.

"I'll start making a list," Lacey said, grabbing a legal pad from off a desk.

"Making a list for what?"

The three of them turned to see Chelsea standing in the doorway, towel-drying her long brown hair.

Seven

Katie exchanged glances quickly with Lacey and Amanda. "For things we want to do while we're here," she said, thinking fast. "I want to go tubing down the river."

"And I'm going to ask if there's any chance I can bungee jump off one of the bridges," Amanda said with a straight face. Katie and Lacey looked at her simultaneously.

"Bungee jump?" Lacey asked drolly.

"It's a possibility," Amanda defended her outlandish suggestion while turning beet red.

Chelsea sat on her bed. "You all don't know how lucky you are. I can't even consider doing such things."

"When you get your heart fixed, you'll be able to do them too," Amanda told her.

Chelsea's lips held a bluish cast, and her breath sounded rapid. Katie remembered vividly what it felt like to have her sick heart pounding so hard that she thought it might jump out of her chest. "Would you like to rest?" Katie asked, concerned for Chelsea.

"If I don't dry my hair right away, it'll turn into a giant frizz ball."

"I'll help you dry it," Katie offered. "It won't take long."

"Um . . . we've got something we have to do," Amanda said. "Don't we, Lacey?"

"I need to talk to Mr. Holloway." Lacey met Katie's gaze with a look that said *I'll handle the arrangements for you.*

Katie was grateful for the way the two others pulled together to set the plan for Chelsea's surprise party into motion. She expected as much from Amanda, but for Lacey, it was downright charitable.

She rummaged in her drawer for her hair dryer and went to work on Chelsea's hair. When she was finished, Chelsea's naturally wavy hair hung in a thick cascade down her back. The color had come back into her face, and her breathing sounded normal. Chelsea said she was tired and opted to lie down for a nap. Katie left her sleeping and headed down to the rec room, wondering all the while how long Chelsea could go on without a transplant. She had noticed how carefully Chelsea conserved her energy. How hesitant she was about joining in activities. She hoped the surprise party was a good idea. That it wouldn't sap her already failing strength. She wished there was something she could do to make Chelsea's day-to-day life less monotonous.

"Happy Birthday!" The group surrounding the foot of the stairs yelled. Katie was partway down, a few steps in front of Chelsea, who stopped, blinked, and stared open-mouthed at the decorated lodge lobby.

"For me?" she asked. "You all did this for me?"

"Are you surprised?" Amanda wanted to know.

Chelsea glanced at Katie, who beamed her a smile and shrugged. "We couldn't let you turn fifteen and not celebrate."

Katie led the rest of the way down the stairs, where the kids and staff waited. She had to hand it to Lacey. She'd done a great job on the arrangements. The place looked like a barn, with bales of hay stacked between tables decorated with red-checked tablecloths. The furniture had been pushed against the walls to create a dance floor in the center of the room, and a bluegrass band tuned up fiddles in front of the fireplace, which sported a gigantic birthday banner.

"I can't believe you did all this for me."

"Any excuse for a party," Mr. Holloway said, offering her his arm. "Come see your cake."

He walked her to a long table holding platters of fried chicken, a bucket of iced sodas, bowls of salads, and a cake decorated with a bucking horse.

"The cake's a little corny, but it was all that the bakery in town could come up with." Lacey sounded apologetic.

"I think it's wonderful." Chelsea's eyes sparkled.

"We've got a minicarnival set up downstairs," someone explained. "Let's eat so we can go play."

Katie had never been a fan of country music, but she decided that the band was outstanding. In no time, the leader had organized a square dance. In her group were Jeff, Amanda, and Lacey and another couple. Amanda pretended that she was only with Jeff, and Jeff could imagine that he was with Lacey.

All Katie worried about was Chelsea, who sat in an easy chair beside the dance floor watching everybody dance. In the girl's face, Katie saw the envy of the dancers. For the physical energy she could never expend.

When it was time to descend to the game room and carnival, Katie offered to take the elevator down with Chelsea. "I probably won't be able to play the games," Chelsea said, sounding apologetic as they rode down in the elevator.

"They're not strenuous."

"I'm not very good at games because I could never participate in them." She licked her lips nervously.

"What are you trying to say?"

The doors slid open, and Katie and Chelsea stepped out. From inside the game room, they heard squeals of laughter as kids tried their luck at the carnival competitions, as well as the standard video game fare.

"I'm just not a competitor," Chelsea explained.

Katie couldn't imagine such a thing. All her life, she'd thrived on competition. "But it's fun to win."

"But I can't win. And the excitement isn't good for me."

"What a thing to say! How do you know you can't win if you don't try?"

Chelsea lowered her gaze. "You don't understand."

But suddenly Katie *did* understand. Chelsea had lived such a protected life for so many years, she'd forgotten what it was to feel adventurous. "You know, every time your heart beats fast it doesn't mean that you're going to pass out. There's a difference between putting pressure on your heart from overexertion and simply having it race because of adrenaline output. Don't be so scared."

Chelsea's gaze had shifted back to Katie's face. "But I am scared," she whispered. "I don't want to flake out in front of all these people."

"I'll be with you. And you're always saying how you wish you could do the things that normal people do."

"But that's the problem—I can't!"

"Wait a minute. There *is* something down here that can give you an adventure safely," Katie said as an idea struck her. "Come with me." Katie led the way into the game room and up to the front of the line of the virtual reality game. "Birthday girl gets to butt," she said, tapping the boy wearing the VR helmet. "Hand it over."

"But I just—"

"Now." Grumbling, the boy climbed out of the cocoon-shaped enclosure and passed the helmet to Katie, who clamped it on Chelsea's head. "This game's three-dimensional, and it has programs to take you anywhere—including Mars."

Chelsea sat stock-still as Katie showed her how to work the controls.

"How'd you like to drive in a Grand Prix road race?" Katie shoved a cartridge for car racing into the control panel. She watched Chelsea's face as the game sprang to life, knowing what Chelsea was experiencing. She'd been transported into another time and place, and with such reality that she'd become a part of it. "I—I can't believe—" Chelsea whispered as the game beeped into activity. "Everything's so *real.*"

"But it's only an illusion," Katie said. "Feel this." She pressed an object into Chelsea's hands.

"Why, it feels just like a real steering wheel."

"But it isn't real," Katie replied. "And that's what makes it perfect for girls with lousy hearts." She stepped back and watched as Chelsea tentatively gripped the wheel. "Have fun," Katie said. "Have a wreck. You can't get hurt, you know."

And for the next half hour, she watched as Chelsea got caught up in a world of make-believe so realistic that it made Chelsea gasp, squeal, and laugh aloud. Katie felt pleased with herself. She'd opened up a realm of adventure that Chelsea could never have experienced any other way. Watching her, Katie realized that for the first time in her life, Chelsea was "running" and "jumping" and "soaring."

She was safe. And she wasn't scared.

While Chelsea continued to play the VR game, Katie tried her hand at some of the carnival games. She went to a booth decorated as a miniature fishing pond, manned by Jeff. He handed her a fishing pole equipped with small magnets for hooks and said, "The fish are rigged with magnets too." He pointed to a child's inflatable pool. "Cast out and see what you snag. The color of the fish determines your prize. Gold ones win you a stuffed turtle."

Katie flexed the pole and readied her aim.

Jeff took a furtive glance around. "We need to talk," he said under his breath.

"About what?"

"I can't get to first base with Lacey. I need some advice."

Inwardly, Katie groaned. She didn't want to be in the middle of this. From the way Amanda looked at him, Katie knew she still pined for him. How could Jeff be so blind? Yet, Katie also knew that Jeff wasn't going to be interested in Amanda the way she would like him to be. "I don't know what to tell you. Try using your imagination. Do something romantic."

"Romantic?"

"It's not a foreign word."

"Maybe you're on to something." Jeff furrowed his brow. "This is going to take some thought."

Katie felt relieved that he was taking the initiative and not depending on her. "Hey," she cried. "I caught a gold fish!" Katie dangled her catch high above the pond.

Jeff fetched her prize and handed it to her. He said, "I might try out some ideas on you."

"It's not me you have to impress."

"But you know her best."

She almost said, *"Nobody knows Lacey,"* but thought better of it. Fortunately, other kids came up to play the fishing game, so Katie slipped away. Deciding to take her stuffed turtle up to her room, she dashed upstairs, ran inside the room, and stopped short.

Amanda was sprawled on her bed, crying, and Lacey was standing over her.

Eight

"WHAT ARE YOU doing to her?" Katie asked sharply, coming immediately to Amanda.

"Don't yell at me," Lacey declared. "I came in here and found her like this. Why do you just assume it's *my* fault?"

"Sorry. That wasn't fair." Katie knelt next to Amanda. "What's wrong? Are you sick?"

"I'm ugly and gross, and no boy's ever going to like me." Amanda turned her tear-stained face toward Katie. "Remember what I told you before? Well, no matter how hard I try, this guy doesn't even know I'm alive."

"This is about some boy?" Lacey blurted out. "You're up here crying your eyes out over some stupid *boy*?"

"That's easy for you to say." Amanda sat upright

on the bed. "You're beautiful, and boys probably fall all over you."

Lacey shook her head. "Not so."

Katie wondered about Lacey's mysterious admission, but now wasn't the time to pursue it. She turned to Amanda. "Look, I know you've been trying your best to get—"

"Don't tell who!" Amanda cried, casting an embarrassed look toward Lacey. "I—I don't want anyone to know."

Lacey crossed her arms and tapped her foot in exasperation. "Oh, really, who cares? I've seen every guy here, and believe me, none are worth my time. And certainly not worth crying over."

Katie snatched a tissue and handed it to Amanda. "Your secret's safe," she promised. "But Lacey's right about one thing—you shouldn't be up here crying when there's a great party going on downstairs. You should see how much Chelsea's enjoying herself with the VR game."

"I'm acting selfish, aren't I? This is supposed to be Chelsea's big party, and I'm ruining it."

"You're not ruining anything," Katie assured Amanda. "It's just that this won't help you any."

"What's the problem anyway?" Lacey wanted to know. "Why don't you just go up and tell the guy you like him?"

"I couldn't. I'd be too embarrassed. And besides, look at me. I'm almost fourteen, and I look like a little girl." Amanda blew her nose and took a swipe at her swollen eyes with the soggy tissue.

"You don't have to look like a kid if you don't want to," Lacey replied.

"What do you mean?"

"Yeah, what do you mean?" Katie wasn't sure she trusted Lacey with Amanda's fragile ego.

"That's why science invented makeup." Lacey put her hands on her hips. "I could fix you up. Make you look a couple of years older in no time."

Katie remembered that Amanda's parents didn't allow her to wear makeup, but before she could remind Lacey, Amanda asked, "You could? You could show me how to look older?"

"In a heartbeat." Lacey dragged Amanda over to the dresser that stored her stash of supplies.

"I don't know—" Katie said, tagging behind.

"I'm not going to make her look X-rated," Lacey said. "Just some subtle changes. It's no big deal."

"Will you help me?" Amanda sounded so hopeful, Katie didn't dare nix the project.

"When I get finished, this guy will be tripping over himself to get to you."

Amanda smiled shyly. "No offense, but no one can work that kind of miracle."

"Lacey Duval can."

"Then go for it," Amanda begged. "Will you stay with us, Katie?"

Katie wasn't sure how to react. She didn't want to spoil anything for Amanda. Or for Lacey. It was the most enthusiastic and interested in anything or anybody Katie had seen Lacey since her arrival at Jenny House.

Lacey ushered Amanda into the bathroom with

one hand and scooped up her tray of cosmetics with the other. Katie padded after them.

"You should restyle your wig," Lacey said, seating Amanda on the closed lid of the toilet. "Let's go with a side part and put a big clip in it." Her fingers worked deftly, and soon Amanda's artificial hair had been swirled to one side and clipped with a colorful barrette. The effect made her look more mature.

"Cool." Amanda said, seeing herself in the mirror. "Now what?"

"Now we get down to basics. Watch carefully, because you've got to learn to do this yourself. It takes practice." She smoothed compact powder on Amanda's face. "You need to find your own special shade, but this will have to do for now."

Katie watched, fascinated as Lacey's fingers, sponges, and brushes went to work. She swept pale pink blusher across Amanda's cheeks, nose, and brow. She dabbed on plum eyeshadow, then artfully smudged it until the color was subdued. She carefully outlined the upper lids of Amanda's already large brown eyes, making them appear even larger.

"You've got great eyes," Lacey remarked. "Play them up."

"Chemo took my lashes and eyebrows," Amanda explained. "They're just now growing back."

"Then we'll work with what's here." Lacey lathered the stubby lashes with black mascara and curled them with an eyelash curler. With feathery strokes, she penciled on new eyebrows. Last, she dug through a pile of lipsticks, trying on several shades before selecting a rosy plum. A layer of gloss went on top of the color. She stepped back and surveyed her handiwork. "So, what do you think?"

Amanda's face broke into a thousand-watt grin when she saw her reflection in the mirror. "I look fabulous! Don't I, Katie?"

"You know you do."

Amanda jumped up. "Thanks a million-zillion, Lacey. I'm going right downstairs and see if anyone notices."

"Wait. You need a spritz of perfume," Lacey declared. But when Amanda picked up a bottle off her own dresser, Lacey snatched it away. "Not that stuff. It's a little girl's perfume. Here, try this." She handed Amanda a fancy spray bottle of a fragrance that Katie had seen featured in only the best department stores.

Amanda spritzed it on, filling the air with the heady aroma of roses and jasmine. "Thanks again."

"I just hope this guy's worth it," Lacey called as Amanda bounded out the door.

When Katie and Lacey were alone, Katie said, "That really was nice of you."

Lacey shrugged self-consciously, as if the act of kindness somehow embarrassed her. "It wasn't anything. I mean, who couldn't like Amanda? She's so" —Lacey hunted for the right word—"enthusiastic."

"You really do know a lot about makeup. How come?"

"I work on the theater productions at school doing makeup. Of course, stage makeup is a whole other thing, but it works on the same principle. It changes flaws. Turns mistakes into assets. Too bad we can't use it on our insides."

Katie had begun to see another side of Lacey and wondered if her attempts at snobbery weren't her way of protecting herself. As far as she could see, there was nothing flawed about Lacey's outward appearance. "You mean you'd use it to cover up your diabetes? But covering it up wouldn't make it go away." Diabetes wasn't something that showed on the outside. Still, the illness *had* to have some effect on Lacey's self-image.

"Life stinks, doesn't it?" Lacey's mouth formed a straight, hard line.

"I don't think so. Maybe it hasn't worked out exactly the way I planned so far, but I love life." She remembered her long days in isolation at the hospital, and her episode of rejection. Her doctor had credited her "unshakable will to live" in part with her survival.

"We're different then, Katie," Lacey said. "I don't see anything at all to recommend living. Especially living with a disease and parents who—" She stopped abruptly.

"Go on."

"Forget it." Lacey flipped her mane of long blond hair. "I'm going downstairs and see how my little makeover is doing."

She spun and left the room, leaving Katie to stare after her, puzzled. And inexplicably afraid for her.

Nine

Katie mulled over her and Lacey's conversation as she walked downstairs. She didn't think she'd ever figure the girl out. One minute, Lacey was helpful and outgoing; the next, pulled back and close-mouthed. Who could deal with such a person?

By now, the lobby below was deserted. The band had packed up and gone, and the food had been removed to the rec room. As Katie started toward the staircase leading down to the sound of laughter, she noticed that the "Happy Birthday" banner had partially fallen. She crossed to the fireplace and rehung it, and when she stepped back, she glanced up at the portrait of Jenny.

The lights in the room had been dimmed, and the flickering flames of the fireplace cast the hearth in a yellow-orange glow. Most of the portrait was smudged by the gloom of shadows, but Katie could make out the pale arch of Jenny's brow and her eyes, with their sad, sweet expression.

"Are you partied out?"

"Mr. Holloway! You startled me."

"Sorry. I was passing through and saw you looking at Jenny." His gaze traveled up toward the face of the portrait. "I often get sidetracked by her picture myself. I can't tell you how many times I've stood here looking at her . . . and remembering."

"She must have been special to you."

"She was." He didn't volunteer any more information, and Katie lacked the courage to pump him for it. He turned to her and smiled. "Your friend Chelsea is totally involved with the virtual reality game. I think you've created a monster."

"I feel sorry for her. She wants so much to participate in life, but isn't physically able. The game seems like a partial solution."

"VR's an interesting concept, all right. I wonder about it, though. It isolates . . . cuts people off from 'actual reality,' which is much more interactive. Are you having a good time this summer?" Richard changed the subject.

"Oh yes. I'm glad I came."

"We are too. You know, you're very good at this."

"At what?"

"At being a friend to the girls in your room."

Katie felt a warm flush creep up her neck. She started to tell him she wasn't very good at all. That so far, she was in the middle of a hopeless love triangle that she couldn't navigate. She glanced back up at the painting of Jenny. "You told me once that she had friends who made a difference in her life. What ever happened to them?"

"Along with Jenny, two others died. I lost track of the fourth. Her name was Kimbra—she'd lost an arm to cancer."

Although she'd never known Jenny's friends, the news depressed Katie. "Jenny signed her One Last Wish letter 'Your Forever Friend.' I read it a million times, trying to figure out who JWC was, and I struggled with those words every time. What's a 'forever friend' to people who are going to die, Mr. Holloway?"

He didn't answer right away, and when he did, his voice was soft and low. "Do you believe in heaven, Katie?"

"I sure do," she said with a small laugh. "When I thought I might die, I wanted to go someplace besides the cold, dark ground. Heaven's supposed to be a pretty special place."

"Jenny believed in heaven too. And she believed that when she got there, her parents would welcome her. I guess to her, a 'forever friend' is one who waits for you in heaven. In Forever. And for Forever."

The explanation sounded beautiful to Katie. And it made perfect sense. Then she remembered her dilemma with Amanda, Jeff, and Lacey. "It's getting through the here and now that's the hard part," she said with a sigh.

"Problems?"

She wanted to bite her tongue. A man as important as Mr. Holloway didn't need to be burdened with silly stuff like crushes and puppy love. "No problems. I mean, not in the real sense of the word. I guess I just want everybody to be happy. Stupid, huh? No one can be happy all the time."

"You're right about that. But I understand where you're coming from. Jenny was that way too. She tried her best to make people happy. That's why giving her money away was important to her."

"I'll never forget the day I got that letter and check. I stashed most of the cash in a savings account after my folks and Josh and I flew home from the Transplant Olympic Games. The money's there for when I need it. For my anti-rejection medications. For college. Although I'm still hoping for a track scholarship, it's nice to know my going to college doesn't depend on whether or not I get one."

The firelight reflected off Richard's blond hair and turned his eyes a golden green. "You know, Katie, of all the kids here, you most remind me of Jenny."

"I do?" His assessment pleased her immensely. Jenny Crawford was fast becoming Katie's ideal.

"Absolutely. She was smart and caring and . . ." His gaze again traveled upward to the portrait, its frame gleaming in the glow of the fire. ". . . and she died too young."

Katie suddenly felt like an intruder, and could think of nothing else to say. That was the bottom line for most of the kids at Jenny House—they were all facing a premature death. "I should get back to the party," she said.

"Go have fun," Mr. Holloway replied.

As she left him, she experienced a deep sense of

melancholy. For him. And for a girl she'd never known, but who had the power to reach beyond the grave and touch all their lives with her gift of love.

"I really got some attention when I came back to the party last night." Amanda started talking before she set her breakfast tray next to Katie's in the cafeteria the next morning. "Some kids didn't even recognize me."

"Did Jeff?"

"He looked real hard at first, then asked, 'Is that you, Mandy?' When I told him yes, he asked what was different—isn't that just like a guy? He knows something's changed, but he acts as if he's gone blind. So I told him Lacey had given me a few makeup pointers, and then he was all ears. He asked me a bunch of questions."

Katie's heart sank as she imagined Jeff's line of questioning. "I can't picture a guy interested in makeup application techniques."

Amanda giggled. "Not that, silly. He wanted to know how Lacey acted about doing it. If we had a good time. If she gave me lessons . . . stuff like that. He asked if I would bring her over so he could talk to her."

"Did you?"

"I was going to. I looked all around for her, but I guess she never came back to the party. Did she stay in the room?"

"No. She left the room right after you did. I came down and wrestled the VR game away from Chelsea. It was way past her bedtime. So, tell me. Did Jeff make a move on you?" Katie half hoped that Amanda would say yes.

"No." Amanda set her glass down and looked momentarily downcast. "But he walked me up to my room after the party was over. We talked and were the last ones to leave." She brightened. "That must mean something, don't you think so, Katie?"

Katie had taken a long morning walk rather than do laps in the pool because she hadn't wanted to run into Jeff, concerned that his version of the night before would be different from Amanda's starry-eyed one. "Don't ask me. Who knows how a guy's brain functions. Except for Josh, I've never even been interested in knowing."

Amanda glanced up at the clock. "Oops . . . I've got an appointment in the clinic for blood work." She stood and picked up her tray. "Listen, do you think you and Chelsea and Lacey can go someplace with me this afternoon? After Chelsea gets up from her nap, I mean."

"Where?"

"Just someplace special I want to show all of you. We'll need the horses, so could the three of you meet me at the stables?"

"I don't know what the others have planned."

"Please, Katie, ask them. If you ask, they'll say yes."

"I don't think I have that much pull—"

"Three o'clock at the stables," Amanda insisted hurriedly. "I've got to go. See you there."

Katie watched Amanda skitter away, wondering what could be so important to her. Later, she asked

Chelsea to come. She hesitated. "I'm not a good rider."

"You did fine before. We'll all be together. This is important to Amanda."

Katie watched Chelsea's internal struggle with fear play across her face before she finally overcame it and said, "All right. Since it's for Mandy."

When she asked Lacey, who was spending the day alone in the room reading, the pretty blond gave her a bored look. "I don't have anything better to do. I guess I can come."

Katie almost replied, *"Don't do us any favors,"* but she swallowed the words. "See you at the stables," she said, and left the room.

Ten

"WHERE ARE YOU taking us?" Lacey called out. Amanda's horse led the way on a path winding ever upward through the lush green woods.

"You'll see!" Amanda replied over her shoulder. "It's not much farther."

"I hope not," Lacey grumbled. "My fanny's getting sore."

Ignoring Lacey's bad humor, Katie glanced at Chelsea. "You doing okay?"

"Fine. Actually, it's good to be out in the fresh air."

"Yeah—a girl can't spend every waking minute with virtual reality," Katie kidded.

"So, I'm slightly addicted," Chelsea said with a laugh. "I can't help myself. When I put on that helmet, when I become a part of another world . . . well, it's so much fun. I feel like I'm on the holodeck of the starship *Enterprise*. I can have fun without exerting myself. I wish I had a VR game at home."

"I understand they're pretty expensive."

"But a lot less scary than thinking about getting a new heart."

Katie sympathized with Chelsea. No matter how much fun she was having this summer, no matter how "lost" she became in a make-believe world, she still had to face the harsh realities of her medical problems. She would still have to "go on the beeper," the process of being on twenty-four-hour call while waiting for a compatible heart to become available. "You can do it," Katie said. "If I did, so can you."

"You're braver than me."

"No . . . I was just more desperate."

"We're here!" Amanda's voice interrupted their conversation. "We'll have to leave the horses and go the rest of the way on foot."

"It's about time." Lacey dismounted, rubbing her backside. "I think it's gone to sleep permanently."

"It'll wake up," Katie assured her as she tethered her horse to a tree and helped Chelsea off her mount.

"Come on," Amanda called. "It's just a little bit farther."

Walking very slowly and holding Chelsea's arm, Katie climbed the last fifty yards. The trees had thinned, and above she saw only a rise in the land that seemingly met the blue sky. When she and Chelsea crawled over a hump, the rise flattened out, and Katie saw that they were standing on a bluff, a flat, jutting chunk of granite that seemed suspended in space. In the distance, as far as she could see, was the deep hazy blue swell of mountains. They reminded her of waves rolling across the land, silent giants as old as time. The bluff dropped off, and hundreds of feet below were woods and trees dressed in the green hues of summer.

Above, the sky was dome-shaped and the sun hovered like a ball over the crests of the Great Smoky Mountains. For a few breathless minutes, the four of them stood staring across the gorge.

"Wow." Katie was the first to speak.

"Isn't it fabulous?" Amanda asked, like a kid showing off an unexpected Christmas gift.

"It's the most beautiful place I've ever seen," Chelsea said, breathing hard from the small exertion.

"Pretty awesome," Lacey added.

"How did you ever find it?" Katie wanted to know.

"Exploring. Sometimes I take a horse for a ride and go exploring on my own."

"Aren't you afraid you'll get lost?" Chelsea asked.

"Course not. The horse knows the way home. If I get confused, I just give him free rein, and he heads straight back to the stables."

"How many times have you come up here alone?" Katie asked.

"Three—not counting the time I discovered it. I tied little scraps of ribbon to mark the trail. Didn't you notice them as we were riding?"

Katie shook her head. "I was talking."

"If you follow the ribbons, you'll get here." She grinned. "I felt like an Indian scout when I did it."

"Indians followed animal tracks," Lacey said. "But I'm impressed, so we won't argue the fine points."

Katie ventured to the edge of the bluff and peeked over. Her gaze tumbled over rocks and trees on the underside of the mountain. "It sure is a long way down."

"Come sit over here." Amanda motioned them to a few rocks gathered in a circle. When they had settled, she said, "I'll bet these rocks were put here by fairies so that they can dance in the light of the full moon."

She giggled, and for an instant, Katie caught her fairy-tale vision. She imagined tiny winged beings sprinkled with gold dust, darting like fireflies around the rock formations.

"I'd prefer someone a bit more life-size up here with me in the moonlight," Lacey declared. She didn't sound sarcastic, and Katie wondered again about Lacey's private life. Katie thought of Josh and realized it would be fun to be with him up here in the moonlight. A summer breeze brought the scent of pine forests and the sweetness of some wild mountain flower, making her miss him all the more.

"But it's just for us," Amanda said. "You've got to promise that you won't show it to anybody else. Not ever."

"Why?" Lacey asked.

"Because I just want it to be for us. Sort of like our private place. A secret that nobody else knows about."

Katie could understand Amanda's wishes. Jenny House seemed to belong to everybody, but the bluff, with the view and the sense of solitude and peacefulness, was unique. Out here, the world looked majestic, ageless, bigger than their problems. She felt dwarfed and insignificant, but not in a negative way. Up here, the rhythms of life merged into a single stream. "I think we can keep this place our secret," she said, looking from face to face.

"No problem by me," Chelsea said.

"I like the idea of not sharing," Lacey added.

"Then it's settled. This belongs to us alone." Amanda grinned. "And any fairies who want to play here."

They sat quietly, listening to the chirp of birds and the silver whisper of the wind. "What now?" Lacey asked.

"We watch the sun go down. It's so beautiful, and after I saw it, I knew I had to bring you three and let you see it too. You're my very best friends in the whole wide world."

Looking around, Katie saw that the others were as touched as she by Amanda's confession. "I feel the same way," she said.

Chelsea asked, "Will it be too dark to get back down?"

"You know how long it stays light in the summertime," Amanda assured her. "We'll be back in time for dinner. Now if you sit tight and watch, you'll see a fantastic light show."

The four of them crowded together, facing west. The great ball of the sun began to dip lower, and the long shadows of afternoon crept along the earth below. The sky flamed crimson and melted into confectionery pink, turning the few clouds into cotton candy puffs. The distant trees began to resemble licorice sticks, and the leaves sweet green icing. When the sun turned scarlet and slid between two distant mountains, Katie was reminded of a cherry resting on mounds of dark ice cream. She watched as the brilliant red ball sank lower, until its rim became a sliver of shimmering light, then disappeared from view.

The sheer beauty of the sight left a lump in her throat. It made no sense. She'd seen hundreds of sunsets, but somehow this one had touched her deep inside and chased away some lonely darkness. Maybe it was because the others were with her. Others who had no promises that they'd see other sunsets. She cleared her throat. "That was beautiful. Thanks for sharing it, Amanda."

Each of them stood, glancing away self-consciously, unable to put her feelings into words. "We should be getting back." It was Lacey who spoke. She started quickly for the horses, but not before Katie saw that her eyes were damp with tears.

Katie thought about chasing her down and finding out what was wrong, but Chelsea took her arm, and Katie knew that the younger girl needed help to return to her horse. Whatever Lacey's problem was would have to wait. The foursome remounted their horses and wound their way back down to Jenny House without speaking.

Over the next two days, the staff and kids talked constantly about the big Fourth of July blow-out. Mr.

Holloway announced plans for a swimming party and picnic at the lake, followed by fireworks. "These are special fireworks," he told them at dinner one evening. "For your eyes only. There'll be a barge in the middle of the lake and plenty of action."

Katie found herself looking forward to it. Ever since their experience on the bluff, she'd felt closer to the other three. And she knew the others felt the same. It was if the rays of that incandescent sinking sun had wrapped them in ribbons of light and bound them together in some unique way. Chelsea acted less fearful. Lacey became friendlier. Amanda was more enthusiastic than ever.

Amanda practiced putting on makeup borrowed from the other three. Katie thought she looked especially adorable on the morning of the picnic, even though she'd had to use a coverup for dark circles under her eyes. "Jeff's got to notice me today," Amanda whispered to Katie.

"If he doesn't, we'll send him up on one of the firework rockets," Katie whispered back.

The intercom buzzed, and Lacey pressed the button. A voice from the front desk said, "Katie, can you come down to the lobby? Something down here needs your attention."

She gave the others a bewildered shrug and bounded out the door. She was halfway down the stairs when she stopped cold and stared wide-eyed at the foot of the carpeted staircase. There stood Josh Martel, looking as if he hadn't slept all night.

Eleven

K ATIE FLEW DOWN the remaining stairs and threw herself into Josh's arms. "It's you! It's really you!"

"Were you expecting someone else?" Josh teased after he kissed her.

"I wasn't expecting *you*. Why are you here? How did you get here? Are you alone?" She fired questions at him while hugging him tightly.

"Let's go outside," Josh said.

Katie glanced around and saw that their reunion had attracted a small crowd. Kids passing through the lobby had stopped to stare, and even staff members had stepped out of their offices to see the source of the commotion. "Hurry," she said, dragging Josh out onto the porch, down the walkway, and into a nearby stand of trees.

Once they were alone, she threw her arms around him again. "I can't believe you're here," she repeated.

"I couldn't stand being away from you for one more day," Josh told her. He swept his hands through her hair and raised her chin with his thumbs.

Staring into the depths of his eyes made Katie feel weak in the knees. She'd known she missed him, but until now, she hadn't realized how *much* she'd missed him. "You look tired." She touched creases around his eyes.

"I drove all night."

"You must be wiped out."

"Not anymore." He kissed her hungrily.

Reluctantly, Katie pulled away. "Come on, there's a bench farther down." Tucking herself under his arm, she walked with him through the hot, green afternoon toward a sitting area farther back in the cool woods. "Tell me everything," she said. "How's everyone back home? And your job? How'd you get off?"

"It's Fourth of July weekend. I asked for two extra days so I could make the drive, nonstop. I left Ann Arbor yesterday morning at six."

"When will you have to leave?"

"I figure I can cut out Monday noon and still make it to work by noon on Tuesday. I'm working the afternoon shift at the paper."

"So we have almost two whole days together. There's a big party tomorrow night. A picnic out at the lake with fireworks."

"Am I invited?"

"I think I can persuade Mr. Holloway to let you stay for it."

"Then the trip was worth it. I get you *and* a party."

Katie shoved his chest playfully. "You should have told me you were coming."

"I wanted to surprise you."

"You sure did that!" Katie snuggled against him when they reached the wrought-iron bench. "You're a wonderful surprise."

"Your folks send their love. Your mom says you should write more often."

Katie felt a twinge of guilt. "I've been so busy around this place, I hardly have time to write. If I do, I write you."

"Good thing. That's all that's kept me going this summer." Josh pulled away and peered down at her. "I've really missed you, Katie."

"Same here." She hugged him. "You should get some sleep."

"Who needs to sleep?"

"You do. I can find a bed where you can crash at Jenny House. Maybe Jeff's room—"

"How's all that stuff going between him and Lacey and Amanda anyway? You've written me so much about them, I feel as if I know them."

"Don't ask. Jeff still pines for Lacey. Amanda longs for Jeff. And Lacey is clueless. Fortunately, Amanda hasn't figured out Jeff's infatuation with Lacey. If she knew, she'd be heartsick."

Josh grinned and shook his head. "And you're playing Ann Landers."

"Don't laugh. This is serious stuff."

"No, this is serious stuff." He leaned down and kissed her until she felt light-headed.

"We'd better go talk to Mr. Holloway," Katie said, when her head had cleared. "He'll have to okay your stay."

"I hope he lets me. The closest motel is a good half hour away. Jenny House is really set off by itself."

"It's a fabulous place, Josh. I'm glad I came."

They walked hand in hand back to the big lodge, and once inside, Katie led the way to the director's office. She could tell by the expression on Richard Holloway's face that news of Josh's arrival had already reached him, and although he was courteous, Katie realized he wasn't too pleased. "I know Josh has come a long way to see you, Katie, but Jenny House isn't for outsiders," Mr. Holloway said, affirming her suspicions.

Clinging to Josh's hand, Katie said, "Josh isn't just my boyfriend on a two-day vacation, Mr. Holloway." Quickly, she told him about how she and Josh had met.

"Katie was given your brother's heart?" Richard Holloway looked incredulous.

Once everything was explained, the director agreed to let Josh remain for two days and join them on the picnic. After they'd left his office, Katie told Josh, "I've got group rap session in thirty minutes."

"What's that?"

"I wrote you about groups. Rapping is when anyone who wants to can sit around with special counselors and talk about their illnesses. Everyone's been to a rap session. Everyone except Lacey. She says talking about it won't make it go away, so why bother."

"She's right, you know."

"Not true! Talking about it, getting your feelings out into the open, really helps you feel better. But Lacey refuses to believe it. She's taking her insulin shots regularly, but otherwise, she refuses to admit she's got a medical problem."

"Too bad." Josh stifled a yawn, and Katie insisted he go up to Jeff's room, get some sleep, and meet her in the cafeteria for supper.

"Tell Jeff I sent you." She raised on her toes and kissed Josh quickly. "Get plenty of rest. You're going to need it."

"Promise?"

She offered a flirtatious smile. "Promise."

By suppertime, everyone at Jenny House knew about Josh's surprise visit. "It's so romantic," Amanda said with a sigh as they sat eating in the cafeteria. "I wish I had a boyfriend like Josh."

"You're lucky, Katie," Chelsea added. "Not only about Josh but about your heart too."

"There are easier ways to meet guys," Katie told them both with a laugh, but she couldn't have been happier.

When Josh joined them at the table, Jeff was with him. She introduced Josh to her friends, and while they ate, he entertained them with stories of his summer job. Katie thoroughly enjoyed hearing how he was spending his summer, but she couldn't help noticing the covert looks Amanda kept giving Jeff. *How could the guy be so blind as not to notice?* she wondered.

The rest of the evening and the following morning flew past. Katie and Josh took a long run through the woods together and swam laps in the pool. They played standard video games, along with a three-way match with Chelsea on the VR game, which Josh proclaimed "awesome."

"This is the most fun I've ever had," Chelsea confided at game's end. Bright spots of color made her cheeks glow, and Katie thought the girl had never looked healthier.

Josh put his hand on Chelsea's shoulder and said, "It's only the beginning. Once you get your new heart, we'll have a foot race."

At noon, a team of horses was hitched to a huge hay wagon, and everyone at Jenny House piled in. They sang songs and stuffed straw down one another's shirts all the way to the lake, and once there, those who felt up to it played a softball game while the staff laid out an old-fashioned picnic including an enormous cake decorated with frothy white frosting, blue and red icing flags, and sparklers.

Katie and Josh took a canoe out on the lake and paddled every twist and turn of the shoreline, and when they were positive they were out of sight of the others, Josh took her in his arms and kissed her. The canoe dipped precariously, but Katie didn't care if it capsized. Kissing Josh was worth getting doused. "Let's go for a walk," Josh urged, shoving the canoe into soft mud along the far shore and climbing out.

"We've got to get back for the fireworks," Katie reminded him. "It'll be dark before long, and we've got a long way to paddle back across the lake."

"We won't be late," he promised, helping her out.

They walked back into the woods, where the air was still and the occasional sound of laughter from the other side of the lake broke the quiet. "I'll never forget today," Katie said. "I'm so glad you came to see me."

He held her close. "Me too. I don't know what I'd do without you, Katie. Whenever I think about last summer, about how you were so close to dying . . ."

She didn't allow him to complete his sentence. "Every day is new, every morning, Josh. I'm glad I got a second chance at life. And after meeting the people here at Jenny House, after making friends with Amanda, Chelsea, and even Lacey, I want all of us to live forever."

He grinned. "Forever's a long time."

She returned his smile. "All right, then at least until we're all old and wrinkled."

Suddenly, Josh silenced her. "Do you hear something?" Katie listened. From nearby, she heard the sound of whispering, but the shadows lengthening through the trees obscured her ability to see who was talking. "Maybe we'd better split," Josh said.

"Maybe we'd better check it out," Katie countered. "Just in case someone needs help." She listened closely, but the whispering had stopped.

"Doesn't sound like anyone's in trouble to me," Josh said.

"We'll just peek," Katie insisted, really curious

now. She sneaked toward the sound of soft giggling and rustling leaves. She rounded a tree trunk and saw two figures in the muddy light. The couple were wrapped in one another's arms and kissing. She felt Josh come up behind her and press against her back.

The couple broke their embrace just as the waning rays of the setting sun shot one final burst through the leaves. Katie's eyes grew wide, and her heart wedged in her throat. For there in the red-gold shimmer of dusk stood Jeff with his arms locked lovingly around Lacey Duval.

Twelve

KATIE FELT GLUED to the ground as shock, disbelief, and anger swept over her. *How could Lacey do this to Amanda?* Josh tugged on the back of her shirt. She glanced over her shoulder and saw him motion for them to slip quietly back into the woods. But she couldn't. She couldn't simply walk away and pretend that she'd seen nothing.

She resisted, and Josh became more insistent. A branch snapped beneath his foot, causing Jeff and Lacey to break their embrace and turn toward the noise. "Who's there?" Jeff demanded.

Feeling like a peeping Tom, Katie cleared her throat and came out from behind a tree. "Don't panic. It's only me and Josh."

Jeff grinned and pulled Lacey closer. "At least it's not a bear."

Lacey stepped away and straightened her clothes. "We . . . um . . . we thought we were alone."

"Surprise," Katie said, none too kindly.

Josh looked apologetic. "We didn't mean to barge in."

"It's getting late anyway," Lacey added. "We need to start back."

"We have a canoe down by the lake," Josh said.

"We walked around," Jeff replied.

Katie wanted to wipe the silly grin off his face, but felt powerless. Hadn't he been trying to get Lacey to notice him for weeks? Suddenly, she turned to Josh. "Why don't you guys take the canoe, and Lacey and I'll walk back together."

Jeff and Josh looked as if she'd lost control of her senses. "Why would we want to do that?" Jeff said.

"I don't think it's a smart idea for us to come out of the woods with lipstick all over our faces," Katie replied, thinking quickly. "We're leaders, and Mr. Holloway might not approve. I don't think we should offend him."

Jeff nodded. "Maybe you're right."

Josh shrugged. "They saw us leave together."

"Please," Katie said.

"All right . . . if you think it's best."

Once the boys had started toward the lake, Katie glared at Lacey and barked, "Come on." She headed down the ever darkening trail, and Lacey had to jog to keep up.

"What's your hurry?" Lacey asked.

"It's getting dark, and I don't want anyone worrying about us."

"We're not babies."

Katie continued her fast clip through the woods surrounding the lake. "I don't want to miss out on the fireworks either."

"Seems as if there's plenty of fireworks right here."

Katie whirled. "What's that supposed to mean?"

Lacey stopped and studied her icily. "It means you're treating me as if I'd committed a crime or something. What's your problem? You've been on my case for weeks about 'joining in,' and the minute I do, you act as if you'd like to drown me."

"I just didn't expect to see you with Jeff, that's all." It occurred to Katie that Lacey really might not know what was going on.

"He's been flirting with me for weeks. I just took him up on it."

"Are you telling me Jeff's a game for you? A fun way to pass the time?"

"What's wrong with that? I'm not interested in marrying the guy. I'm just having a little fun."

Katie felt like exploding. Instead, she took a couple of deep breaths before saying, "He likes you, Lacey. Don't play with his feelings. Don't jerk him around."

"Who are you? Mother Teresa? For crying out loud, I took a walk with him in the woods and let him kiss me. Stop treating me like a criminal!"

Lacey walked off in a huff, and all at once, Katie realized that she had overreacted. No wonder Lacey was peeved at her. She hurried to catch up. "Wait a minute. I didn't mean to come across so bad. I'm really not mad at you."

"You could have fooled me." Lacey's voice sounded thick, as if she might be struggling to hold back tears.

"There's just a lot going on you may not know about."

"Like what?"

By now, they had rounded the edge of the lake, and Katie could see the glow of a bonfire ahead. Everyone at Jenny House was gathered around, roasting marshmallows and waiting for the fireworks to begin. In the middle of the lake, she could make out a barge from where the fiery spectacle would be launched, and coming through the dark water, she saw Josh and Jeff paddling the canoe, aiming for the shoreline and bonfire.

"Wait, Lacey. Before we get back to the party, I need to tell you something."

Lacey turned, but refused to look Katie in the eye. She crossed her arms and stared down at the ground. "So tell me."

Katie's mouth felt dry as cotton. "It'll mean breaking a promise I made to someone."

"Are you going to tell me or not?"

"Remember how you helped Amanda with her makeup? How much she was aiming to impress some guy?"

Lacey's head rose, and her gaze locked onto Katie's. Slowly, Katie saw the dawn of realization spread across Lacey's pretty face. "Are you telling me the guy she's been trying to impress is Jeff?" Katie nodded. "I didn't know." Lacey looked stricken. "You've got to believe me. I had no idea."

"I believe you," Katie said. All the fight had left her, and she felt drained and weighed down by a jumble of emotions. A part of her had expected Lacey to be blasé about the situation. To shrug it off.

"I wouldn't do anything to hurt Amanda. I honestly wouldn't. Not her," Lacey added insistently.

"I said I believe you."

"I don't think Jeff has a clue about the way Amanda feels," Lacey said.

"She doesn't want him to know."

"So what should I do about him?" Lacey asked.

"Do you like him or not?"

"I like him all right. I don't go around kissing just any guy. But I don't like him enough to hurt Amanda."

"But he likes you."

"I'd rather hurt him than her," Lacey said, running her hand through her long blond hair. "I told you once that I don't like hanging around sick people. And so the last thing I want is a guy who's a hemophiliac. Besides, he lives out west, and so after this summer, what are the odds I'll ever see him again?"

Katie could find no fault with Lacey's logic, even though it rubbed her wrong. "Jeff won't understand your dumping him. And we can't force him to like Amanda either."

"That's not my problem," Lacey said. "And right now, I'm tired of talking about it. I'm going to find Amanda and sit with her for the fireworks. Are you coming?"

The abruptness of Lacey's change from concern to indifference baffled Katie. Would she ever be able to figure out this girl? "I'll join you, but let me grab Josh first."

Katie and Josh sat with her roommates on a blanket spread out facing the lake. Jeff tagged along, and the hopeful expression on Amanda's face when he asked to sit with them made Katie's heart ache.

"I think you should sit with the guys in your room," Lacey said coolly.

Jeff stopped short. "But I wanted to be with you all."

Amanda scooted aside and patted the blanket beside her. "We'll make room. There's plenty for all of us."

As Jeff settled in between Amanda and Lacey, Lacey stood. "Then I'll go sit with the guys from your room," she said. And without a backward glance, she walked away. Jeff stared, speechless, but only Katie realized how deeply he'd been wounded. Jeff gave her a questioning look, but she avoided his gaze and pressed herself against Josh's side, wishing that the ground would swallow her up and put her out of her misery.

The sound of popping and the sight of a starburst of color in the night sky overhead made her look upward. She felt Josh's arm tighten around her waist and his lips brush her ear. "I love you," he whispered, and at that moment, nothing else mattered to her. Tomorrow would have to sort itself out. Tonight the world was ablaze with color, and she was safe in Josh's arms.

*   *   *

Early the next morning, Katie and Josh packed up his car, then went for a long walk. "I don't want you to leave," she told him.

"And I don't want to go. But let's look on the bright side—there's more of the summer behind us than is left in front of us."

"True. I'll be coming home in about six weeks."

"I'll try to hold out."

When they returned from their walk, they went to the cafeteria for breakfast. The smell of waffles and warm maple syrup made Katie's stomach grumble. "Some of the drugs I take every day make me extra hungry," she explained by way of apology.

Josh laughed. "I don't take any medicine, and I could eat the paint off the walls."

They got their food and found a table to themselves. "Listen, don't let this stuff with Jeff and Lacey and Amanda get you down," Josh said.

"Has Jeff said anything to you?"

"He tried to. Tried to ask why he and Lacey were going great until you took a walk with Lacey. I told him you had nothing to do with it and he'd better not hassle you."

Katie groaned. "I was afraid he'd think it was all my fault."

"You let Lacey set him straight. She doesn't strike me as the type to mince words."

"She isn't. But I hate to see Jeff hurt. He's a really nice guy."

"Somebody's got to lose, Katie. Don't get in the middle of it."

She started to say she already was in the middle

when Lacey came rushing up to their table. Her face looked white, her eyes frightened. "Katie, come quick!"

"What's wrong?"

"It's Amanda. Mr. Holloway just had her taken to the hospital."

Thirteen

"CALM DOWN, PLEASE. I can't answer any questions with all of you talking to me at once," Mr. Holloway insisted, standing behind his desk facing Katie, Lacey, and Chelsea.

"We're calm," Katie said, knowing it was a lie. She glanced at the others, who with their eyes gave her permission to be the spokesperson. "We just want to know what's happened to Amanda."

"She didn't collapse or anything," Richard assured them. "But the results of her most recent blood work looked bad. I called her family, who called her doctor, and he wanted her taken over to the hospital that's overseeing the welfare of Jenny House kids. She'll have the best of care until her parents can get here."

"If her parents are coming right away, then it must be pretty bad," Katie commented.

"It's standard procedure," Richard said. "Once they confer with the doctors, a decision will be made as to what to do."

"We want to go see her," Chelsea blurted out.

"As soon as we can," Lacey added.

"I don't know—"

"Please." Katie interrupted. "She's all alone until her family arrives. I know she's scared."

"One of our staff is with her."

"It's not the same as having us. We're her friends."

Richard glanced from one to the other, and Katie crossed her fingers and held her breath. "It's an hour's drive."

"Can't someone from the staff take us and wait with us until her parents come?"

"They have to make flight arrangements. You could be at the hospital most of the day. I have your welfare to consider too."

Katie felt that she and Lacey would be fine, but she was concerned about Chelsea, whose bad heart left her with little reserve energy. "Maybe we all don't have to go," she suggested.

"You're not leaving me out," Chelsea insisted. "I'll be at a hospital, for crying out loud. What safer place?"

Richard took a deep breath and nodded. "Come on. I'll drive the three of you and send the staffer back here. We'll wait together until Amanda's parents arrive."

*　　*　　*

The hospital was part of the North Carolina university system. It was an enormous redbrick building, surrounded by asphalt parking lots that shimmered with heat waves. Once inside, Katie saw clusters of people scurrying across the busy lobby. Many were dressed in white lab coats, but most reminded her of college kids back in Ann Arbor. Thinking of home brought Josh to her mind. Because of the rush to see Amanda, she'd given him a hurried good-bye kiss before he'd driven away. He'd promised to call to check on news of Amanda.

As Katie and her friends crossed to a gleaming row of elevators, Richard explained, "Because this is a teaching hospital, there're classrooms and several auditoriums on the lower floors. This place has some of the newest and best medical equipment around. Plenty of fine medical minds here too."

Katie knew he was trying to assure them that Amanda was in good hands, but all she wanted was to see her friend with her own eyes. They took an elevator up to the oncology floor and followed directions given at the nurses' station to Amanda's room. Richard paused to speak with the Jenny House staff member outside Amanda's door while the girls hurried inside.

Each of the four beds held a patient. Amanda's was nearest a window. She lay curled into a ball under the sheets. Her wig had been removed, and a bright bandanna was wrapped around her head. A few wisps of hair poked out. As they approached, Amanda scooted up and grabbed a tissue. Katie could tell that she'd been crying hard. "What are you all doing here?" Amanda asked in a thick, quivery voice.

"You didn't think we'd let them take you off without saying good-bye, did you?" Katie said.

Fresh tears brimmed in Amanda's eyes. "Oh, Katie, I want to go back to Jenny House."

"It's just for a little while, Mandy," Chelsea offered.

"But they've called my parents. Don't you see? My leukemia's come back."

"That's bad, isn't it?"

"This is my third relapse. During my last one, they told me that every relapse makes it harder to retain another remission. I've only been out of the hospital six months since my last problem. This is awful, Katie. The worst."

"That's why you're in a hospital," Lacey declared. "So that these brilliant doctors can figure out what to do next for you."

"A bone marrow transplant is my only hope. I've been entered in the national bone marrow directory for a year, and they've not found a compatible donor for me yet."

Katie understood completely what it was to wait around for a donor. To jump every time the phone rang, wondering if it was the hospital. To wear a beeper and pray it would go off, announcing that a donor had been found. "Don't get discouraged."

Amanda blew her nose. "How long can you stay?"

"Mr. Holloway said we can wait until your parents arrive."

"You won't have to be alone for a single minute," Chelsea added.

"But you all have stuff to do at Jenny House." Amanda peeked at Lacey. "And I know how much you all hate hospitals."

"Well, it's not so bad," Lacey said. "Especially when you're only a visitor. We'll manage for a while —case the place for you. Make sure they treat you like a VIP."

Amanda managed a smile. "I'm a Very Important Patient, all right. I've already had a team of interns check me over and poke me."

"Any cute ones?"

Amanda's smile broadened. "A few. But none as cute as Jeff."

"You like Jeff?" Chelsea asked, giving Katie an I-told-you-so look. Katie recalled that Chelsea had been the first to spot Amanda's interest in the guy.

"It doesn't matter now if you know," Amanda said. "Yes, I like him, and he's been nice to me, but I was beginning to catch on that he didn't like me. Not like a girlfriend. No guy ever does."

Katie and Lacey exchanged glances. "Are you giving up?" Lacey asked. "Honestly, didn't I teach you anything? A girl doesn't just give up over every little setback."

"I'd say that knowing he doesn't like me and landing in the hospital are two major setbacks," Amanda replied. Suddenly, she punched her pillow and buried her face in her hands. "This stinks! It really stinks."

Katie felt helpless. "Everyone back at Jenny House

is worried about you. And everyone is pulling for you. Lots of them said to tell you hi."

"Especially Jeff," Lacey blurted out.

Amanda glanced up at her. "He did?"

Katie wished she could clamp her hand over Lacey's mouth. Giving Amanda false hope about Jeff wasn't smart. "Is there anything you want from the room?" she asked, attempting to change the subject.

"Not really. I guess as soon as my parents come and make the arrangements, I'll have to go back home. They'll come and clean everything out of the room." Amanda's expression turned forlorn. "I'll really miss you all. You're my best friends. You all understand what it's like being sick. My friends back home never did."

"Hey, you aren't out of here yet." The comment came from Richard Holloway, who'd come alongside Amanda's bed. His smile was warm and friendly.

"You know I don't want to leave," Amanda told him. "Jenny House is the best place in the whole world."

"That's nice of you to say. And once you get back on your feet, I want you to come back. We're open year-round."

Just then, a team of doctors swept into the room. One announced, "Sorry to break up the party, but we have to take Amanda downstairs for testing."

"How long will these tests take?" Richard asked.

"A couple of hours."

Katie hoped Mr. Holloway wouldn't make them leave. "I'll treat all of you to lunch," he said, allaying her fears. "There's a nice place in town. Real cloth napkins," he joked. "Then we'll come back."

"We'll see you soon," Katie told Amanda. Once they were out of the room, she caught Lacey's arm and let the others go on ahead. "I'm wondering if it's wise to make Amanda think Jeff feels something for her when he doesn't."

"Don't worry about it. That's what she needed to hear. Didn't you see how she perked up when I told her?"

"Yes, but it wasn't exactly the truth."

"Jeff will do whatever I ask him," Lacey insisted. "And it's not like we're being cruel or anything. Right now, Amanda needs hope. And something to keep her mind off what's happening to her. I think Jeff is the perfect diversion."

"You can't go around manipulating people's lives, Lacey."

Lacey jutted her chin and pulled her arm from Katie's grasp. "Don't preach to me. I know what I'm doing. It won't hurt either Amanda or Jeff. I know he'll cooperate, and it'll make her feel better. It's the only thing I can do for her right now, so I'm doing it."

"Hurry up," Richard called. He was holding open the elevator doors. Lacey dashed forward, and Katie had to jog to keep up. A part of her felt what Lacey was doing wasn't right, but she was forced to concede that under the circumstances, it didn't seem wrong either. She told herself she'd go along with the charade. Just so long as no one got hurt.

Fourteen

KATIE NOTICED THAT none of them ate much lunch even though the restaurant was every bit as fancy as Mr. Holloway had promised. She watched Chelsea pick at an elegant salad and Lacey nibble on gourmet soup and crackers. Mr. Holloway noticed too. He said, "You three should eat. I don't know when we'll be getting back to Jenny House tonight."

"Every hospital has a cafeteria," Chelsea said listlessly.

"And since we've all eaten in them, we know that's not where we want to dine tonight, don't we?" he asked.

Katie offered a wan smile at his attempt to lighten their moods. "If Amanda goes home soon, can we keep in touch with her?" she asked. "You know, like call her from Jenny House every couple of days."

"I don't see why not," Richard said.

"I could help pay for the calls," she added, thinking of her remaining Wish money.

"That won't be necessary. We'll cover the costs. Where is her home anyway? I know I should remember, but I'm trying to keep track of so many . . ." He didn't finish his apology.

"Kansas," Chelsea said.

"Like Dorothy and the Wizard of Oz," Lacey commented tonelessly. "You know—over the rainbow."

The comment brought Amanda's bright, cheerful face to Katie's mind, her bubbly personality and enthusiasm. A persistent lump clogged her throat, and she sniffed and pushed her plate aside. "I'm finished," she said.

"Ditto," Lacey said.

Chelsea nodded in agreement.

Mr. Holloway didn't insist anyone eat any more. "Then let's head back."

Silently, they drove to the hospital. Katie gazed absently out the window, wishing with all her heart that they could be headed over the rainbow, instead of into the land of reality that awaited them behind the gleaming glass doors of medical science.

When they got to Amanda's room, her parents were with her, looking worried and haggard. They hovered around her bed, as if their presence might ward off the gremlins of cancer that had attacked her. In her bed, Amanda looked pale and weak. When her parents stepped into the hall to talk to Mr. Holloway, Katie, Chelsea, and Lacey clustered around her.

"Was it awful?" Chelsea asked. "The tests, I mean."

" 'Fraid so," Amanda whispered. "Have you ever had someone punch a needle into your spine? I hate the spinal taps worst of all. They give me such a headache." Her words were so faint, Katie had to lean in to hear them.

Lacey took Amanda's hand. "The fiends. Shall I have them shot?"

Even in her pain, Amanda managed a smile. "You made a joke. Shot by a needle, shot by a gun . . . get it?"

Lacey blinked back tears. "I guess I did make a funny."

"Mr. Holloway said he'll bring us to visit tomorrow," Katie said, smoothing Amanda's forehead like a mother trying to comfort a child.

"That'll be good. I don't know what else they're planning for me." Her eyes were closed, and a tear slipped from the corner, unnerving Katie.

"You feel better," Chelsea ordered fiercely. "I want to see you smiling when we come back."

"Tell Jeff hello for me," Amanda whispered.

Lacey caught Katie's eye and told Amanda, "I'll take care of it personally."

Mr. Holloway signaled them from the doorway, and so they said their good-byes and let Amanda's parents take their places with their daughter.

Outside, darkness had fallen. Once they were in the car and driving along the expressway, Richard said, "I know all of you are concerned about Amanda, but unfortunately there's not a whole lot to report yet. Results of the lab work will be studied before decisions can be made."

"What kinds of decisions?" Katie wanted to know.

"Whether to fly her home or keep her where she is."

"You mean she might be able to stay?" Katie felt a flare of hope and glanced at Lacey and Chelsea on either side of her in the backseat.

"It's a possibility."

Katie felt Chelsea squeeze her hand and Lacey nudge her. "And we can go see her every day?"

"I'll see to it that a car is made available to shuttle you to and from the hospital. And while I don't think that every kid at Jenny House should tag along, it will be okay for a few of her closest friends to accompany you. Just not all at once."

Katie could almost hear the wheels turning inside Lacey's head after Mr. Holloway's pronouncement. She told herself to have a serious talk with her about the plans Katie knew Lacey was concocting concerning Jeff and Amanda. "Don't worry. I'll make sure everyone understands and that things go smoothly," Katie told the director.

"That would be a good sign, wouldn't it?" Chelsea asked. "I mean, if they leave her right where she is, things must not be as serious as they thought."

"Perhaps," Richard said. His tone was noncommittal, but Katie could see his eyes in the rearview mirror. They looked troubled. And very sad.

"Amanda likes *me*? But she's just a kid. I never gave her any reason to think that I liked her—I mean I *like* her, and I'm really sorry she's in the hospital. But I've never liked her in a boy-girl way. How did she get that idea?" Jeff asked Lacey and Katie once they cornered him at Jenny House.

On their arrival, Chelsea had been totally exhausted and had gone straight to the room. But Katie and Lacey had fielded questions about Amanda from the other kids and grabbed Jeff for a private talk in one of the smaller lounges next to the game room.

"Never mind how she got the idea, she just has it," Lacey replied.

Katie almost reminded her that it was Lacey who'd fueled Amanda's hopes and made implications about Jeff's having deeper feelings for the younger girl. Instead, she ignored Lacey and said, "Jeff, it doesn't matter how Amanda got her crush on you. Believe me, she has one."

"Why didn't you say something to me before?"

Katie felt her cheeks redden as Jeff stared hard at her. She knew he was remembering all the times he'd asked her to fix him up with Lacey. He was obviously feeling like a fool, feeling that Katie had somehow deceived him. "She begged me not to, so I didn't," Katie explained. "I was just being her friend."

"I thought you were my friend too."

His words stung, and Katie squirmed.

Lacey blurted, "For crying out loud! Will the two of you resolve that issue later? We've got plans to make."

Jeff leaned back into his chair and studied Lacey. "What kinds of plans?"

"I think you should go and see her," Lacey said.

"I would have done that anyway."

"I mean, see her and act like you care."

"I do care."

Lacey looked exasperated, and Katie tried to make herself invisible. "You know what I mean," Lacey snapped. "*Really* care. Like a guy would care about a special girlfriend."

Katie heard herself say, "Jeff, it would mean a lot to Amanda. Right now, she's hurting and depressed and hopeless. You're the only one who could change her mental outlook."

Jeff glanced from one to the other. "Let me get this straight. The two of you have decided that for Amanda's emotional health, I should fake undying love."

Katie flushed. It sounded so cold and artificial the way he said it. For an instant, she was angry with Lacey for sucking her into the whole mess. But the moment passed when she realized that she didn't totally disagree with his analysis. If only he could see Amanda and how bad she was hurting! "Look, I know you think we're using you—"

"And lying to Amanda," he added.

"But it's not what you think." Stubbornly, Katie pressed on. "Come to the hospital tomorrow and visit her. You'll see how she reacts when you're there, and then you'll understand why we're doing this for her. And why we're asking you to do it for her."

"That sounds fair," Lacey declared. "Can't you give it a trial run? What could it hurt?"

Before Jeff could answer, one of the younger boys

poked his head through the doorway and shouted, "Hey, Katie, there's a Josh on the phone for you."

Katie jumped up. She'd forgotten that Josh was headed home and that he'd promised to call for an update. "Tell him I'll be right there." She turned toward Jeff and asked, "What do you say?"

"All right," he said slowly, but Katie saw the set line of his jaw and a gleam of anger in his eyes as he answered. Lacey stood as if to leave the room with Katie, and he grabbed her wrist. "Just a minute. I want to talk to you."

Lacey looked helplessly at Katie, who knew her presence was no longer wanted in the room. She shrugged and stepped out the door. As far as she was concerned, Lacey was on her own now.

"What do you want?" Katie heard Lacey ask.

As she stepped into the corridor, Katie heard Jeff say, "What about us?"

"Us?" Lacey repeated.

Katie paused.

"Us on the Fourth of July," Jeff said. His voice sounded cold. "Us on our walk. Us kissing in the dark. What did all that mean? Or do you kiss every guy who tells you you're beautiful and makes an idiot out of himself over you?"

Katie heard Lacey reply, "So long as Amanda's sick, there isn't any 'us.' There's only *her*."

"And then?" Jeff asked.

"And then we'll all go home." Lacey used her frostiest voice. "You to Colorado and me to Miami. End of story."

Katie bolted down the hall, making it to the stairwell just as Lacey rushed from the room. Katie heard Lacey go to the elevator and punch the button. She pressed herself flat against the wall, feeling guilty for having lingered and heard more than she should. She held her breath until she heard the elevator doors slide open. She heard the doors begin to close and almost breathed a sigh of relief until the sudden sound of Lacey bursting into tears filled the quiet hall. The sound caused Katie's stomach to constrict. Why was Lacey crying? She'd gotten Jeff to do exactly what she wanted, and now tears?

The sound grew muffled as the elevator doors closed completely, but the echo haunted Katie all the way up the flight of stairs.

Fifteen

THE NEXT MORNING, WHEN KATIE AND LACEY arrived at Amanda's room, she was sitting up in bed, fiddling with her wig. She smiled when she saw them, but Katie could see dark circles under her eyes and skin that looked pinched and drawn. "I'm glad you're here, Lacey," Amanda said. "I can't do a thing with my hair."

Lacey flashed a big smile and held out her hands. "Give it to me, and I'll see what I can do."

"How are you feeling?" Katie asked.

"The terrible headache's gone, but I won't lie—I still feel rotten. Where's Chelsea?"

"Yesterday wiped her out, so she's resting. But she says she'll be here this afternoon to visit."

"And that's not all," Lacey said as she combed and styled the wig. "Jeff's coming too."

"Are you serious?" Amanda's eyes grew wide. "But he can't! I mean, look at me! I look awful."

"Have no fear, Lacey's here," Lacey announced, giving the wig a final pat. "There, all done. Why don't you put it on later—closer to Jeff's visit?"

"Stick it on my wig stand for now." She pointed to a Styrofoam head on the dresser. A vase of red roses also stood atop the dresser. "From my daddy," she said, when Katie asked about the flowers.

"Where are your parents anyway?" Katie asked.

"Making arrangements to move to North Carolina until I can go home."

"You mean, you're staying?" Katie felt a rekindling of hope that Amanda would be treated and sent back to Jenny House.

"The doctors had a long talk with me and my parents earlier this morning. Since the prospects for a bone marrow transplant don't seem too good, and since the usual chemos aren't working for me, they want to put me on some new experimental drug," Amanda explained.

Katie and Lacey exchanged long looks. "You mean you're going to become a guinea pig?" Lacey asked.

"They call it devo chemo—developmental chemotherapy," Amanda replied. "This hospital is one of a few that has permission from the government to use this stuff. It's made from tree bark."

"Go on," Lacey said as if Amanda were putting her on.

"I'm not kidding."

Katie recalled her physical therapist's telling her how one of the anti-rejection drugs she was taking had been discovered as a microbe in a Norwegian soil sample, and how, later, a scientist had developed it into a powerful immune-suppressant drug used for transplant patients. "It's not so strange," she told Lacey. "There are people who think that all diseases can be treated by natural compounds already in our earth and oceans. All we have to do is find them. Just think about the insulin you take."

Lacey rolled her eyes in bored contempt. "I'd rather not, so spare me the science lecture." She turned back toward Amanda. "So when are they starting you on this tree bark stuff?"

"Tomorrow." Amanda sighed and stared out the window longingly. "But they have to put me into isolation to do it."

Katie's heart squeezed. She knew all about isolation, having spent weeks in it herself. The room would be no more than a big box without windows. It would be completely sterile—cleaned and filtered to remove all bacteria, which could kill if it touched a patient with a weakened immune system. It would have an airlock—double doors to keep out people and further guarantee against bacterial invasion. All visitors would have to wear sterile gowns, masks, and head coverings. To Katie, isolation was like being buried alive. "You ever been in isolation?" Katie asked carefully, hoping her aversion wasn't showing.

"Once, when I was ten," Amanda said. "I hated it."

Lacey put her hands on her hips and snapped, "So you're isolated. What's the big deal? They'll still let us in to visit you, won't they?"

"Maybe," Amanda said. "It depends."

"Well you'll have a phone, won't you?"

"Probably."

"Then there you go—they can't keep us away."

Amanda smiled. "You two are great friends."

Katie felt her throat tighten, but refused to let Amanda see how upset she was. Lacey began rummaging in a drawer. "Here's the bag of tricks—a makeup supply. I think I should start putting this stuff on for you," Lacey said breezily. Katie could see that Lacey was also struggling to maintain control of her emotions.

"You know I don't have much," Amanda said. "Just the stuff you've given me."

"I've got more in my purse." Lacey pointed where it lay on the floor. "My survival kit. Your parents aren't going to get weird about this, are they? I mean, they *will* let you wear makeup now that you're stuck in this place."

"I don't think it'll be a problem," Amanda told her. "They pretty much want to help however they can." She turned toward Katie. "I heard my daddy crying last night. He didn't know I was awake, but I was. He was standing by the window, and Mom was asleep on a cot. It's awful hearing him cry. I wanted to tell him I was all right, but I didn't want him to know I heard him."

Katie nodded solemnly. She figured they were all going to shed some tears watching Amanda go through the next several weeks. "I hope they can find a nice place to stay," Amanda murmured. "The doctor told us that the hospital has some special apartments set aside in a nearby apartment building. It's for out-of-town families who have people stuck here for treatments."

"How civilized," Katie remarked without humor.

Amanda turned to Lacey. "All right, let's get started on my makeup. I've seen myself in the mirror, and you've got your work cut out for you."

Lacey bustled over to the bed and started laying out her bottles and compacts and makeup brushes. "When I finish, you'll look like a princess."

"I can't believe Jeff's coming to see me," Amanda said quietly. "Just thinking about it makes me feel better."

Lacey glanced quickly at Katie and set right to work.

Jeff and Chelsea arrived around one. Amanda's parents still hadn't returned, which suited Katie fine. She wanted Amanda to have Jeff's undivided attention. "Hi," he said, coming to the side of her bed.

"Hi," she returned shyly. Katie thought Lacey had done a superb job of making Amanda's skin look rosy and glowing.

He pointed to the bag hanging from the IV stand, with the long tube stretching to the back of Amanda's hand, where the IV needle was inserted. "Lunch?" he asked.

She giggled. "Hamburgers and french fries are a lot better."

"Tell you what, when you get out of here, I'll take you to the nearest hamburger stand."

"Promise?"

"It's a firm date."

Amanda's eyes fairly danced. Chelsea cleared her throat. "Remember me?"

Amanda looked flustered, then reached out and gave Chelsea a hug. "How are *you* feeling?"

Katie was touched. Only Amanda would think to inquire about someone else's health while she was the one so sick. "I'm great. But lonely. I don't have anyone to talk to before I fall asleep at night."

"But I don't have to listen to you two whispering in the dark," Lacey said in good-humored jesting.

Katie was well aware that Jeff was refusing to acknowledge either her or Lacey. He pointedly ignored them both. "I brought you a present," he told Amanda.

Delight spread over her face. "You did? What?"

He placed a small paper sack in her hands. "Open it and find out."

Katie saw that Amanda's fingers were trembling as she opened the sack and pulled out a small, tissue-wrapped object. She unfolded the tissue and lifted a colorful paper mobile of the sun, the moon, a sprinkle of stars, and a rainbow. Each dangled from a separate string and fluttered when Amanda puffed on it. "This is so neat," she said.

"Here's what you do with it." Jeff took it, looped it over the top of her IV stand, and let it dangle and sway. "Now you can see the lights of the sky without ever leaving your room. A nurse taught me this trick when I was just a little kid. I had to go into the hospital for transfusions whenever I had a bleeding episode, and boy, did I hate it!"

Amanda nodded in agreement. Jeff continued. "It

was bad enough being stuck with needles, but being confined to bed for days on end was the worst part. So, this nurse taught me how to 'escape' by hanging mobiles on my IV stand. I would lie there and watch them move for hours. There was nothing else to do." He grinned. "So, now you can go over the rainbow if you want."

A feeling of déjà vu crept over Katie with Jeff's last words. Hadn't it been only yesterday that she'd wished Amanda could escape to the same place?

"I love it," Amanda said, gazing up at the mobile. "Thanks."

He bowed from the waist. "There are others where that came from."

"Where's that?"

"From me." Jeff's words made Amanda smile her beautiful smile, and Katie wanted to throw her own arms around him for making Amanda so happy. Yet she knew better than to say a word.

It was Lacey who broke the spell. "I need to leave for a minute," she said.

Katie took one look at her and went cold with alarm. Lacey's face was the color of paste, and she looked wobbly. Katie knew instantly that Lacey was having an insulin reaction. She swiftly went to Lacey's side and put her arm around her, saying as nonchalantly as possible, "I'll go with you. We've hogged Amanda all morning. It's time to share her. Back in a bit," she called over her shoulder as she helped Lacey out of the room as discreetly as she could.

Katie got them to a lounge area and settled Lacey

on the sofa. By now, Lacey's breath was coming in gasps, and she was as white as a sheet. "How can I help?" Katie asked urgently.

"S-sugar . . ." Lacey mumbled.

Katie tore over to a table where someone had set up a coffee station. She grabbed several packets of sugar, ran back to Lacey, ripped them open and sprinkled the contents on her friend's tongue. Lacey's head lolled back against the sofa, but she sucked on the sugar, and slowly, color began to return to her cheeks.

Katie's heart pounded. She took Lacey's hand. It felt cold and clammy and was trembling, but after several minutes, the shaking stopped. Lacey raised her head. Although her eyes looked glassy, she managed a weak smile. "I guess I forgot to eat lunch."

Katie's voice quivered as she spoke. "I'll run down to the cafeteria and buy you something."

"Thanks for covering for me," Lacey said.

Katie stood and dug in her pocket for the five-dollar bill she'd stuffed in that morning. "No problem."

Suddenly, Jeff's voice cut sharply through the air. "All right, you two. What are you up to now?"

Sixteen

LACEY DUCKED HER head, and Katie felt an intense desire to protect her. "We're not up to anything," she said. "We were just leaving you and Amanda alone together."

"Don't you mean Amanda, Chelsea, and me?" Jeff's eyes narrowed as he studied Lacey's face. "You look like you don't feel good."

"I'm perfectly fine."

Jeff stepped around Katie, lowered himself to the sofa, and took Lacey's hand. "You're cold as ice." She tried to pull away, but he refused to let go. "What's wrong?" His tone softened.

"A little insulin reaction," Katie blurted, although Lacey shot her a look that said to hush up. "Well, there's no use pretending," Katie exclaimed. "It's a fact of your life."

"Are you all right?" Jeff's voice was edged with concern.

"I told you, I'm fine. I forgot to eat lunch, and my blood sugar got a little low. It's nothing."

Katie saw that Lacey's face was pinched with pain, and she realized that the reaction had given her friend a headache. "I was headed down to the cafeteria for a sandwich," she told Jeff.

Jeff stood. "I'll go. Stay with her, Katie."

"But Amanda—" Lacey started.

"Will be fine until I get back," he interrupted.

"I'm not an invalid," Lacey insisted. "I'm not really sick."

"You have diabetes," Jeff said. "It has its own set of built-in problems. Stop pretending nothing's wrong with you."

"And you stop treating me like a baby."

"Then stop acting like one."

Katie felt caught in their crossfire. "Just go get her something to eat," she interjected. "She needs food."

When he'd hurried off down the hall, Lacey flopped her head back against the sofa and said through clenched teeth, "I *hate* diabetes! I really hate it."

Katie saw a tear of frustration squeeze from the corner of Lacey's eye. "I understand," she said in total empathy. "I remember how I hated it when my heart got the virus that destroyed it. All my life, I was perfectly healthy, and then—BAM!—without warning, this virus moves in and eats away at my heart. I couldn't even walk across the room without gasping for air."

Lacey sniffed. "It must have been awful."

"They told me I was going to die. I was only sixteen. I sure didn't want to die."

"That's what going to happen to Chelsea, isn't it?"

"Without a transplant, probably so," Katie said ruefully.

"Life stinks!"

"No, it doesn't," Katie replied emphatically. "Life is wonderful. Especially when you have to fight so hard for it."

Lacey stared up at the ceiling, her mouth forming a bitter line. "If only I'd never come here this summer."

Her comment shocked Katie. Of course, Lacey had been a pain at first, but she'd turned out to be a good friend to Amanda, and in spite of everything, Katie liked Lacey immensely. "You seemed to be having a better time lately," she said. "I thought you were enjoying being at Jenny House."

"That's the problem." She closed her eyes. "I didn't want to care about any of you. I really tried hard not to. But ever since that day Amanda took us up on the mountain to watch the sunset . . ."

So, Lacey had felt something extraordinary that day too, Katie thought. "Well, like it or not, you're here," Katie told her. "We're all in this together."

"Why did Amanda have to get sick?" Lacey whispered. "Why did Jeff—" Lacey stopped abruptly.

"Go on," Katie said.

"Nothing."

Katie studied her closely, then felt a dawning sensation spread through her. "Wait a minute—"

Before she could complete her thought, Jeff came loping up to them. "I hope you like tuna salad. It's all they had." He thrust a cellophane-wrapped sandwich into Lacey's hands. "And I got you a soda too."

"Thanks," Lacey mumbled. He shifted awkwardly from foot to foot while she pulled off the wrapper. She snapped, "I can eat this without an audience, you know."

"Feel free," Jeff countered. He glared at her, and for a moment, Katie thought he was going to yell. He didn't, but with much control, he turned toward Katie and said, "Katie, she's all yours. Stay with her—in case she chokes. I'll be in Amanda's room." He turned on his heel and marched off down the hall.

Taken aback, Katie could only mumble, "What's wrong with the two of you? Why do you always end up fighting?"

"Nothing's wrong," Lacey insisted. She gathered up the sandwich and soda. "I'm going to eat this in the bathroom."

"But—"

"I'll meet you in Amanda's room *after* he's gone."

Stunned, Katie watched Lacey hurry to the ladies' room. She shook her head, attempting to clear it, to make sense of Lacey's renewed hostility. "I'll never figure that girl out," she muttered under her breath, and forcing Lacey and Jeff out of her mind, she returned to visit with Amanda.

"Do you really think he likes me?" Amanda asked when she was alone with Katie, Chelsea, and Lacey.

"He stayed around all afternoon, didn't he?" Lacey

asked. "You think a guy like Jeff hasn't got anything better to do? Of course he likes you." Katie flashed Lacey a look that said to cool it, but the pretty blonde ignored her. "He's stuck on you."

"And just when things are looking up for me, I have to go into isolation. This is so unfair." Amanda pounded her small fists into the mattress.

"The mobile is dynamite," Chelsea commented, fingering the rainbow. "When I get stuck in the hospital again, will you make me one?"

"Who do I look like—an expert in origami?" Amanda wore a small pout on her mouth.

They all burst out laughing, and when Amanda's parents arrived at the room a few minutes later, they were still making jokes and giggling. When it was time to leave, Amanda's mother walked Katie, Lacey, and Chelsea to the elevator, took each of their hands, and said, "Thank you for being such good friends to our little girl. I can't tell you what it means to us to see her smiling."

Katie noticed the worry lines on Mrs. Burdick's face. "This new drug *is* supposed to do the trick, isn't it?" Katie asked. "I mean, after a few weeks on it, she'll be better again, won't she?"

Mrs. Burdick leaned wearily against the wall. "Frankly, we don't know what to expect. They told us that it'll make her very sick. You see, it's highly toxic."

"Toxic? But that's like poisonous."

"In a way it is poisonous. The trick is to poison the cancer cells and leave the other cells as unaffected as possible."

"How can they do that?" Chelsea wanted to know.

"I don't believe they can. Everything gets poisoned." Mrs. Burdick rubbed her temples. "I don't mean to depress you three. I only want you to be prepared."

"Prepared for what?" Katie asked, feeling a chill go through her.

Mrs. Burdick blinked back tears and said, "For anything."

By the time they arrived back at Jenny House, Chelsea was too tired to eat dinner in the cafeteria, so Katie brought a plate for her up to the room. Lacey disappeared immediately after dinner, and once Chelsea was settled, Katie felt wound up in knots. She changed into her running shoes and started out the front door. On the porch, Jeff caught her arm. "Where're you off to?" he asked.

"I need to run. It'll be light for another couple of hours, so I'm running the woods trail."

"Did Lacey recover from her reaction?"

"She's fine."

"Listen, I didn't mean to shout at her today." He shook his head and clenched his fists. "That girl drives me nuts. She's cold. She's hot. She's indifferent. I don't know how to act around her."

"I don't have any answers for you, Jeff." Katie felt sorry for him. And sorry for her part in deceiving Amanda at his expense. She liked Jeff and wanted to make things right between the two of them again. "I'm sorry that I got involved in this whole scheme with Amanda. I didn't mean for it to get out of hand. But she really likes you, Jeff, and because she thinks you care about her . . . well, it makes her feel better. And gives her something to think about besides what the doctors are doing to her."

"Katie, that's not a problem. I admit, I was ticked off when I first found out how you and Lacey were manipulating everything, but after being with Amanda today, I'm not mad about it. Poor kid." He ran his hand through his thick blond hair. "She's got a lousy few weeks in front of her. If I can help take her mind off of it, then I will. Besides, she's so sweet, how could I not like her?"

Katie felt a wave of relief. Only a guy like Jeff, a guy who'd lain in a hospital bed himself, could be so understanding. "When this is all over with, you can write her a couple of times, then do a slow fade-out. She'll get busy in school and get interested in a guy more her age. You'll see. It'll work out."

Jeff smiled. "You're such an optimist, Katie O'Roark."

She returned his smile. "Friends?" She held out her hand.

"Friends," he said, shaking it. "Have a good run."

She waved, and jogged toward the woods. She ran up the trail, enjoying the exhilaration of physical exercise. A summer breeze cooled her skin and rippled through her hair. She wished Josh were with her, and remembered the times he'd met her at the high school track and helped her train for the Transplant Olympics. She missed him terribly and found herself almost looking forward to school's starting. Even though it would mean leaving Jenny House behind.

Katie rounded a bend in the trail and stopped. A

sound had caught her attention. Puzzled, she held her breath and waited. There! It came again. Back in the trees, someone was crying. Carefully, Katie threaded her way through the thicket, following the sound of soft sobbing the way a bird follows a trail of bread crumbs.

She stepped into a clearing, and there, huddled on the ground, she saw Lacey. Her face was buried in her hands, and she was crying as if her heart were breaking in half.

Seventeen

~∽~

"LACEY!" KATIE CRIED. "What's wrong?" She jogged over and stooped down on the grassy ground.

Lacey scrambled to wipe her eyes with her fingertips. "I—I thought I was alone," she mumbled, her voice thick with tears. "I really want to be by myself."

"No way," Katie declared, suddenly angry. "You always brush me off and sneak away. Well, not this time, Lacey Duval. Like it or not, I'm your friend, and I'm not going to get lost. This time, you're going to talk to me."

Lacey looked shocked by Katie's outburst, but she didn't pull back. "There's nothing to say."

Katie released an exasperated squeal and grabbed Lacey's shoulder. "Listen up! I know something's wrong. Something more than being broken up about

Amanda. Talk to me, Lacey. Tell me what's going on."

Lacey took a deep, shuddering breath, and a look of helpless resignation crossed her face. "It's Jeff, of course."

"Jeff? What about him?" A strange feeling stole over Katie, and she saw herself, Lacey, and Jeff again in the hospital waiting room earlier that afternoon. The tension had been so thick, she could have cut it with a knife, but because of Lacey's insulin reaction, because of concentrating on Amanda, she'd let her suspicions about Lacey and Jeff slip away. "He means something to you, doesn't he?" she asked.

Lacey nodded. "I'd give anything in the world if he didn't, but he does."

"Hey, he's a great guy. What's so wrong with your caring about him?" Lacey only shrugged. Katie searched for a way to keep her talking. "Is it because of Amanda?"

"A little."

"Are you afraid that if you act like you care about him, he'll ignore her? Jeff won't do that. Amanda's important to him, and he'd never hurt her."

"I'm all mixed up inside. I should have never let him kiss me."

Katie smiled. "Fireworks, huh?"

"Rockets," Lacey confessed.

"Fireworks and rockets are nice," Katie kidded. "Is that the way you feel about Josh?"

Lacey's question made Katie pause. Josh was the first real boyfriend she'd ever had, and he'd come to her in such a peculiar way. By now, being with Josh was comfortable and familiar. It was knowing what he was thinking before he even spoke. It was anticipating his moods and feelings whenever they were together. "Maybe not rockets," Katie admitted. "I don't know . . . it's just that Josh has always been there for me. I can't imagine my life without him."

"Well, my life was perfectly fine until Jeff wandered into it."

"He hardly wandered. He's had his eye on you since day one."

"What?" Lacey sat bolt upright. "You mean the two of you have discussed me? Talked about his feelings for me?"

Katie felt her face flame red and wished she could have eaten her words. She mumbled, "He wanted me to fix the two of you up."

"Well, thank you very much for sharing, Katie."

Katie didn't want Lacey to pull her usual stunt of running off instead of talking things out. She held fast to Lacey's elbow. "I owe you an explanation. First of all, it wasn't a conspiracy. I was caught in the middle. Amanda liked him. He liked you. You liked—" She shrugged. "Who knows? Until Josh and I stumbled across the two of you on the Fourth of July, I was refusing to help him at all in your behalf. I told him he was on his own."

"He made out all right." Lacey's tone was sarcastic.

"Stop acting that way. Face it, the thing you're most mad about isn't that I knew something you didn't, but that you responded to Jeff. That you care for him." Katie could tell she'd scored points by the expression on Lacey's face. She continued. "What you have to figure out now is what you're going to do about it."

"Nothing!" Lacey said emphatically. "Absolutely nothing."

She stood, and Katie bolted upward beside her. "Explain."

"It's difficult to explain."

"I have an IQ higher than a mushroom. Try me."

Lacey turned to face Katie. Her expression was determined and lofty, the one that she used to push people away from her. "I will *not* be involved with a guy who's sick. Back home in Miami, all my friends are healthy and fine. My diabetes doesn't get in the way because I don't allow it to. I want to be around regular kids. Kids who aren't worried about medicine and hospitals and doctors and sickness!" She fairly spat out the last word. "Kids who aren't going to die!"

Lacey's anger made Katie step back, as if she'd been physically shoved. "You're not going to give Jeff a chance because he's a hemophiliac? That's dumb. And prejudiced," she added hotly. "And you've made me feel like a freak too."

Lacey tossed her mane of long blond hair. "Grow up, Katie. We're *all* freaks."

Too stunned to respond, Katie watched Lacey stalk off into the surrounding woods. She stood alone while around her, shadows crept and lengthened until they closed off the daylight altogether. And although the evening air was heavy and damp with summer humidity, she shivered.

*   *   *

That night, Lacey surrounded herself with a wall of silence and went to bed early. Katie was grateful that poor Chelsea was too tired to notice Lacey's behavior. As it was, Katie was concerned enough about Chelsea. Going to see Amanda daily was taking its toll on her. She determined to talk Chelsea into visiting on a less regular basis, or she'd be ending up in the hospital too. But it was Lacey Katie wanted to deal with first. So the next morning, when Chelsea had gone into the bathroom for her shower, Katie sat down on Lacey's bed and shook her shoulder.

"Wake up, Lacey. Let's talk." Lacey rolled away from her. "Don't try to fake me out," Katie said. "I know you're awake, and I'm not going away until we talk, so turn over and listen up."

Slowly, Lacey rolled to face Katie. Her eyes looked red and puffy. "Leave me alone."

"No way. I want you to know that I don't hold anything you said to me last evening against you." She thought she saw the slightest expression of relief flash across Lacey's face. "It'll take a lot more than being called a freak to chase me away."

"I—I'm sorry—"

Katie held up her hand. "Not that it didn't hurt my feelings. But I'm tough, so that's not what really got to me. What blows my mind is that you think *you're* a freak because you're less than perfect like the 'friends' you talk about back home. Haven't you heard? Nobody's perfect."

"You know what I mean. Not everybody's sick. Or diseased."

Katie winced. "You still don't get it, do you? That's

what Jenny House is all about. So we can come and be with people just like us. People who feel like we do. It was what Jenny wanted, you know."

"You mean the girl in the painting?"

Katie nodded. "Mr. Holloway's told me some things about her. Personally, I think there might have been something going on between them before she got sick. It was years ago that she died, but I can tell that she's still pretty special to him."

"As Amanda would say, 'How romantic.'"

"Don't be sarcastic. The point is, Jenny wanted to give kids like us a chance to have some fun and an opportunity to be supportive of one another. Even when someone acts as if she doesn't want support." Katie arched her eyebrows and drilled her gaze into Lacey's so that she'd get her point.

"I care about you and Amanda and Chelsea," Lacey declared. "You are all special friends to me." She dropped her gaze. "Even though I don't always show it."

"But you *do* show it. You helped Amanda with her makeup, didn't you? You gave Jeff to Amanda even though you really like him. That was pretty unselfish. It was nice of you."

"Nice? Don't say that. I can't go around having people think I'm nice. Do you want to ruin my reputation?" Lacey raked her fingers through her tangled hair and put on a shaky smile.

Katie returned a smile. "I'll promise to keep it a secret."

"Keep what a secret?" Chelsea asked. She'd come out of the bathroom.

Katie and Lacey glanced at her, and both smiled. "That deep down Lacey is a marshmallow," Katie said.

Chelsea waved her hand. "Everyone knows that."

"Who is spreading such lies?" Lacey demanded, jumping out of bed. "I'll scratch their eyes out."

Chelsea grinned. "I'll tell you on the way to visit Amanda."

Katie cleared her throat. "Uh—maybe you should take it easy today."

"No way. I know my limits, Katie. I know I'm pushing them now, but I want to see Amanda as much as I can. I promise to come back here after lunch and rest all afternoon," she added when Katie opened her mouth to argue. "I—I just want to be around her. I don't know why, but somehow I feel like I might not get another chance."

Katie nodded, understanding perfectly Chelsea's reasoning. She and Amanda were walking side by side down the same dark road, each in her own way. And no one could ever predict what tomorrow might bring. No one.

Eighteen

$\sim$

OVER THE NEXT few days, Katie, Lacey, Chelsea, and Jeff had to visit her in isolation one at a time. They had to suit up in sterile gowns, gloves, and masks and couldn't stay longer than ten minutes. Katie hated going into the room, because it reminded her too much of her experience, yet she never let Amanda know it.

The experimental drug was in a bag hung on an IV pole, and ran through tubing into an infusion pump attached to more tubing and a shunt embedded in Amanda's chest near her collarbone. Jeff's mobile hung beside the bag, adding the only bit of color to the pale green and white world. The first couple of days, Amanda tolerated the drug without side effects and her spirits remained high. But by day three, she felt nauseated, and the next day, no one could visit with her except her parents because she was vomiting almost constantly.

"This junk is supposed to help her!" Lacey ranted while pacing the floor of the waiting room. They had come at the end of the week, only to be told Amanda was still too sick to receive visitors.

"Calm down," Jeff said. "They said there would be a period of adjustment."

Katie chewed her lip nervously. "She's awfully sick, Jeff."

"I'm scared," Chelsea admitted. "I thought she'd be better by now."

"Well, I think we should do something," Lacey insisted.

"Like what? Knock down the door and rip out her IV?" Jeff retorted.

Katie hated to hear the two of them sniping at each other. Especially when she knew how they felt about one another. But Lacey wasn't about to drop her guard around Jeff, and it was obvious that Jeff wasn't going to allow himself to pine over Lacey. "Can't you two stop arguing for one minute?" Katie asked. "Do you want the nurses to throw us out?"

"Sorry," Jeff mumbled.

"Same," Lacey said, turning toward the TV set that was broadcasting some game show on the other side of the room.

When Amanda's mother came into the waiting room, they clustered around her. She looked so worn and haggard, Katie almost cried. "She any better?" Katie asked, knowing the answer even before Mrs. Burdick shook her head.

"Mandy hurts so bad. She's so sick. She keeps begging the doctor to make her well. She wants to know when they're going to stop torturing her." Mrs. Burdick wrung her hands. "I can't stand seeing her suffer like this. How do I know we're doing the right thing? She's in agony, and I feel like we've signed her over to some stupid experimental program that's slowly killing her." She bent her head and wept softly in her hands.

Jeff put his arms around her. "You're doing the only thing you can, Mrs. Burdick. I remember when I was about thirteen, and I had a bad bleed. They thought I was dying. My parents had to make some hard choices, but in the end, it turned out they made the right ones."

Katie saw a look of pure anguish on Lacey's face as Jeff told his story.

"I guess there is no right or wrong in this." Mrs. Burdick's voice sounded muffled. "I mean, there really weren't any alternatives."

Katie and her friends returned to Jenny House that day without seeing Amanda. That evening, the night air turned chilly, and a fire was lit in the huge stone fireplace. Katie sat alone on the sofa and stared morosely into the flames.

"You all right?" Mr. Holloway asked, coming and sitting beside her.

She wiped moisture off her cheeks. "Not really."

"Anything I can do to help?"

"Can you make Amanda well?"

" 'Fraid not." He glanced up at the portrait of

Jenny. "No more than I could have helped way back when."

His sadness was almost tangible, and Katie didn't want him to dwell on it. "It's August. You know what that means? We'll all have to go home soon. I can't stand to think about going off and leaving Amanda in that awful hospital."

"Jenny House will remain open. We have others coming in, even through the school year. You can come back any time you want, even if it's just for a weekend."

Katie thought of her life back in Ann Arbor. In another month, school would start—her long lost senior year. And Josh was waiting for her. Although the rest of her life was waiting to happen, this summer and Jenny House would forever be a part of her. "I feel like someone's put me on hold, like on the telephone. I keep waiting for them to come back on the line, but they don't."

Richard chuckled, deep in his throat. "Haven't we all felt that way at one time or another? Look here, I have something for you and your roommates." He reached into the breast pocket of his suit and pulled out an envelope.

"What's this?"

"Copies of a photograph taken on the night of Chelsea's birthday party."

Katie pulled one out and held it up to catch the firelight. In it, she and Lacey, Chelsea, and Amanda were standing in front of the stone hearth. Amanda was mugging outrageously, Chelsea looked radiant, Lacey beautiful, and she happy. Behind them was the birthday banner, and above them, Jenny gazed serenely down from her portrait. "I'd forgotten this was taken." She smiled. "That sure was a great party." It had also been the night Lacey had taught Amanda makeup tricks so that she could attract Jeff's attention.

"I thought you could give copies to the others. I've already had one sent to the hospital. It'll be sterilized properly and put in Amanda's room," Richard explained.

"You did?" His thoughtfulness touched her.

"I know what friends mean to one another. Jenny taught me that."

"I'm going to give these to Chelsea and Lacey right now." Katie jumped up from the sofa.

"I think Chelsea's down in the game room."

"Thanks. These are really special." Katie hurried downstairs, and in the game room, she found Chelsea tethered to the virtual reality helmet. Katie interrupted the game to give her the photo.

"I love it," Chelsea said, setting down the helmet and gazing at the picture. "We all look so happy." Her smile faded. "Not like now."

"Stop thinking bad thoughts," Katie said. "This is going to end up all right."

"Do you really think so?"

Katie was torn with anxiety, but she didn't want to spread it to Chelsea. "So what adventure are you having?" She changed the subject.

"I'm off to the moon."

"How is it?"

"It's a nice place to visit, but . . ."

". . . but you wouldn't want to live there," Katie finished with a giggle.

Chelsea smiled. "Oh, Katie, I'm going to miss this game. Whenever I put on this helmet, I can go anyplace. My heart condition isn't a problem. My health doesn't matter. I'm going to miss Jenny House so much. And you."

"Me too. But VR *is* only a game. When you get your new heart, you won't need the game."

Chelsea shook her head. "Every time I think about it, I get so scared."

"I know. I was scared too. But it worked out for me, and I think it'll work out for you also."

"Did you know that the closest transplant center for me is the same one you went to?"

"It is?"

"I asked my mom when she called one time where I'd be sent, and she checked it out with my doctor. That's what he told her. If I get approved for the transplant program, then I'll be sent to Ann Arbor."

Katie felt a peculiar sense of excitement about the news. "I know that place like the back of my hand. If you come, I'll be able to be with you through the whole thing."

"And you *would* stay with me, wouldn't you?"

"You need to ask?"

Chelsea's smile faded, and a look of apprehension crossed her face. "It's so much to think about. An operation. A new heart. Being normal." She gave Katie a shy glance. "So, tell me, will I get a guy like Josh in the deal?"

"I can't guarantee that," Katie said with a laugh.

"But I have lots of friends, and you'll get to meet them all."

"Except for you, Lacey, and Amanda, I've never had any real friends. I mean, I've always been sick, and I couldn't go to school. So, how was I going to make any?"

The long and lonely life Chelsea had led bothered Katie. When she thought about the differences between their heart problems, she was glad that she'd had fifteen years of normal life before being struck by disaster. "Well, it's like my One Last Wish letter said," Katie told Chelsea. "Friends can't make the pain go away, but it's nice to know someone understands what we're going through."

"You mean misery loves company?"

Katie laughed. "Something like that." She put her arm around Chelsea's shoulder. "Come on, let's go find Lacey and give her her photograph. I want the three of us to be together tonight."

"Me too," Chelsea agreed. "And we'll put the pictures on Amanda's bed and pretend she's with us also."

"She will be," Katie said. "We'll wish her here. Just like in the movies. Just like in a dream."

When they heard the news, everyone was upset. Amanda's condition had worsened over the weekend. She had become septic as bacteria invaded her body in spite of all precautions. Katie learned that their friend's heartbeat had grown irregular and that a crash cart had been placed in her room in case her heart stopped and she needed to be resuscitated. Katie and her friends practically lived in the hospital waiting room. And then, a week before they were all to return home, Amanda's parents made a startling announcement.

"We're taking her off the experimental drug," they said.

Nineteen

❧

"Off the program?" Katie asked, dumbstruck.

Mrs. Burdick reached out and took her husband's hand. "Amanda's suffering horribly, and nothing is making her better. We discussed it with her doctors this morning, and we're refusing further treatment."

"But we thought it was her only hope," Lacey blurted.

"As it turns out, this treatment isn't as successful with Amanda's type of cancer as it is with other types. We knew it was a long shot all along."

This part was news to Katie, and it sent a cold, sinking sensation through her stomach. *A long shot all along* . . . The words echoed in her head.

"She begged us to stop," Mr. Burdick continued quietly. His face looked desolate. "She said, 'It's not helping, Daddy, and I hurt so bad. Please, please make them stop.' I can't keep watching them do this to my little girl."

"But—" Lacey began again.

Katie reached out and silenced her with a touch. "We want to go in and see her."

"That's what she wants too," Mrs. Burdick replied. "She wants all of you to come at once."

"All of us? Can we do that?" Chelsea's voice quavered with her question.

"You'll have to gown up, but yes, it's all right now." Mrs. Burdick's expression was serious, but Katie thought she somehow looked peaceful. It was as if now that the decision was made to end the experimental treatments, she'd found new courage to face what lay ahead for her family.

Katie and the others dressed in the sterile gowns in the interlock, and except for the rustle of the paper coverings, there was silence. Just before they stepped into Amanda's room, Katie said, "No crying. We have to be brave, and we can't start blubbering and make her unhappy or scared. Agreed?"

The others nodded.

Katie led the way into the room. New pieces of equipment lined the walls, including what she recognized as a respirator. She wished she didn't know so much about medical things. She crossed the room to Amanda's bed. Amanda lay curled in a fetal position, so small and wan on the stark white sheets that it took Katie's breath away. Her skin was bright yellow, jaundiced from a failing liver. Her thin hair looked stuck to her head, her cheeks were sunken, and her breath came in small gasps.

Jeff crouched down and picked up Amanda's hand. "Hi," he whispered. "How's my girl?"

Amanda's eyes opened slowly and focused on his face. "Not so good," she whispered back.

"We're here, Mandy," Chelsea said. "The whole gang of us."

Amanda rolled over and struggled to straighten out under the covers. Katie reached beneath the blankets and helped her. "Pillow," Amanda said. Katie tucked an extra pillow under Amanda's head to help prop her up. "Thank you." Amanda glanced at each of them, stopping her gaze to take in every face. "I've sure missed you guys."

Katie fought against the lump in her throat, and when she was certain she could control her voice, she said, "It's just not the same at Jenny House without you."

"I don't think I'll be going back, though."

"I can't see why," Lacey announced crisply. "Take it from me, this place has nothing to recommend it."

Amanda managed a smile. "I'm sorry I look so bad. You taught me better. And I'll try and shape up for the next time I see you." Her words sounded slurred, and Katie knew that the pain medication was affecting her speech. She recalled the sensation vividly. It had been like trying to talk with a mouthful of peanut butter. She only hoped that the medication was doing its job and that Amanda wasn't hurting.

Jeff twined his fingers through Amanda's. "You look fine to me."

"Am I still your girlfriend?"

"Absolutely." He flashed a cocky smile. "What a dumb question."

"Then you'll do me a favor?"

"Anything."

Amanda slowly unlaced her fingers from his and held his hand toward Lacey. "I want you to take special care of my friend for me. Take her out for that hamburger you promised to me."

Lacey recoiled, as if she'd been stung. "I can get my own dates," she declared. "You don't have to hand me your rejects."

Katie winced and wished Lacey would hush up. Jeff reached out and seized Lacey's hand, so that Amanda could see it. He shot Lacey a withering look, and she clamped her lips tightly.

Amanda turned her gaze toward Jeff. "She acts tough, but she's not. You take care of her for me, all right?"

"It's a deal."

Lacey could no longer hold in her tears, and she began to shake with sobs. She threw her arms around Amanda. "I—I'm s-s-sorry . . ." Panic-stricken, she looked at Katie, backed away, and fled the room.

"Go on," Amanda told Jeff.

He kissed her forehead and said, "I love you, Mandy."

When he was gone, the room seemed hollow, and some of the light went out of Amanda's eyes. She closed them, as if gathering her strength, and then reached out to Chelsea. "Don't let what's happening to me make you a coward."

"I don't know what you mean."

"This dying stuff is hard work, Chelsea. If you have a chance to live, go for it."

Katie recalled when she'd almost rejected her transplanted heart. When she'd lain in the hospital, unaware of the passage of time, occasionally thinking, *So this is what dying feels like*. Amanda was right, it was hard to let go of life. Katie had never been sure how she'd managed not to do it. Maybe it was having Josh with her. Maybe it was simply her pure Irish stubbornness, but somehow she had held on. "Don't give up," she urged Amanda.

Chelsea looked pale and her lips bluish, yet her voice was strong when she said, "I'm no quitter. And I'm not a coward, especially after this summer. I rode a horse to a picnic, for gosh sakes! Plus, I shared a bathroom with Lacey. Now, that's bravery."

Her joke made Amanda smile, but Katie could see that Chelsea was having trouble keeping herself together. She gave Katie an apologetic glance and added, "I think I need to sit down. I'll meet you in the waiting room."

"Go on."

Chelsea squeezed Amanda's hand. "See you soon."

Katie started to follow her out, but Amanda caught her arm. "Don't leave yet."

Katie paused. "What is it?"

"I need to say some things to you." Amanda's voice was so weak, Katie had to place her ear next to Amanda's mouth in order to hear her. "You were my very best friend, Katie. More than a friend. A sister. Remember how we both always wanted a sister?"

Katie's throat was clogged with tears, and all she could do was nod.

"Thank you for giving me the best summer ever."

"I didn't do anything—"

"Thank you for Jeff too."

"Jeff?"

Katie waited while Amanda struggled for air. "I always knew he wanted Lacey," she whispered.

Katie straightened, feeling flustered. "That's not so, Mandy. He likes you. He really does. *You're* his girlfriend. You've seen how he and Lacey get on together. It's like World War Three between them. They positively hate—"

Amanda tugged on Katie's arm to halt her flow of words. "It's okay. I didn't mind pretending I was his real girlfriend. It helped when I was alone. When I hurt so much. I thought of him and how wonderful it was to have him near me. Love is good medicine." For an instant, the bright, impish smile that belonged uniquely to Amanda flashed across her face. "Don't tell them I knew."

Katie returned her smile. The pretense was gone between them. So, Amanda had known the truth all along. . . . Yet, the charade had been something Jeff and Lacey had wanted to give to Amanda, so Amanda allowed them to believe they had given it. Katie nodded. "It'll be our secret. And I know what you mean about love. Sometimes I think Josh pulled me through by sheer force of his will."

Amanda's eyelids drooped. "This medicine makes me so sleepy."

"I'll let you sleep, then."

"I don't really want to. I want to stay awake."

"It's all right. We'll be back tomorrow."

"If tomorrow comes," she whispered as her eyes closed and she drifted away into the twilight land Katie had visited herself one summer. When, like Amanda's, *her* life had been hanging by a thread.

Early the next morning, Amanda slipped into a coma, where she hovered for days. Mr. Holloway personally took Katie and her friends to visit each day, then brought them back to Jenny House for meals and sleeping.

Each day, Katie eased into Amanda's room to see her stretched out on her bed as if she were only asleep. Katie listened to the hum of machines, the hiss of a respirator, the beep of a heart monitor. She spun the colorful mobile still hanging on the IV stand, now holding bags of saline solution and nutrients. She willed Amanda to open her eyes. To grace them with her sunny smile. She talked to her, knowing that hearing was the last of the five senses to leave a person.

"Dying's hard work," Amanda had told Chelsea. "Live!" Katie whispered to her friend.

When Katie returned to Jenny House, she began packing up her things for her return trip to Ann Arbor, now less than three days away. Her parents had called to say they were driving down to North Carolina to pick her up. But understanding her involvement with Amanda, they'd rented a hotel room and promised to wait "until your friend wakes up," as her father had put it. She thought his choice of words touching.

Josh called her to say he was wrapping up his job and would be waiting in her driveway when she returned. "Gramps is going to cook us dinner," he said. "And he's not a bad cook either."

Josh's enthusiasm reminded her that life went on in spite of what was happening at the hospital to Amanda. She continued to pack slowly, moving around Chelsea and Lacey like a sleepwalker. Each of them seemed to be in a state of suspended animation, trapped between staying and going. Caught, like insects in some elaborate cosmic web.

After lunch that same afternoon, Richard Holloway appeared at their doorway. Katie stopped her packing. Lacey dropped an armful of already folded clothes. Chelsea eased herself down on her bed. "What is it?" Katie asked, her heart thudding with dread. "What's wrong?"

"Amanda died less than thirty minutes ago," he said with a catch in his voice. "She's with my Jenny now."

Twenty

A WAVE OF nausea passed through Katie. She heard Chelsea start to cry. Lacey said not a single word. She simply brushed past Mr. Holloway and left the room.

"I'm sorry," Richard said. "I wish there had been some other way to tell you. I wish I hadn't had to tell you at all."

"How are her mom and dad?" Katie asked.

"Better than I expected. It's hard waiting for someone to die. You feel helpless."

Katie realized that he was telling her as much about Jenny's death as about Amanda's. "What happens now?"

"Her parents are having her body flown back to Kansas for burial. They've asked the staff to pack her things and send them along. Unless, of course, you all would rather do it."

Katie shook her head. She could barely stand to look at Amanda's corner of the room as it was. She knew she'd never be able to touch Amanda's possessions and store them away in boxes. She tried to imagine which was going to be harder: to see Amanda's things where her hands had last placed them, or to see her space empty, as if she'd never existed at all.

Once Richard had gone, Katie sat beside Chelsea, who continued to weep. "I've never known anybody who died before, Katie. I mean, Mandy was only thirteen. It isn't fair."

Katie cried right along with Chelsea, feeling anger mix with her sorrow. It *wasn't* fair. "But aren't we glad we got to know her? She was pretty special."

Chelsea reached for a tissue. "Where did Lacey go?"

"Who knows."

"I wish she were here. I want us all to be together."

Irritation toward Lacey allowed Katie to curb her grief. Why did that girl always run off? Didn't she realize this was hard on all of them? "Maybe she went to tell Jeff," Katie suggested.

"Jeff! Do you think he knows?" Chelsea twisted her soggy tissue. "I really think he cared a lot for Amanda in the end."

"I know he did." Katie moved off the bed. "I better go look for him. If Lacey's with him, I'll bring her back."

"You won't leave me for long, will you?"

"Not too long," Katie promised.

She splashed cold water on her face, grabbed some tissues, and went downstairs. She found Jeff in the game room, playing Ping-Pong with one of the younger boys. He took one look at Katie, dropped the paddle, and walked over to her.

"What's happened?" She told him about Amanda and saw his eyes fill with moisture. "We knew it was coming, but I wasn't ready for it. When I saw her yesterday, I thought I felt her squeeze my hand. I guess it was just my imagination." He put his arms around Katie and let her cry on his shoulder. "You know, Katie, I really did love her."

Katie blew her nose. "We all did." She took a long, shuddering breath and pulled away from Jeff. "I came looking for Lacey. Have you seen her?"

"Not today. But then Miss Keep Away hasn't been exactly available to me. I don't know why she hates me so much."

"She doesn't," Katie said. "She's all mixed up inside. And she took Amanda's sickness pretty hard. Harder than any of us in a way. I think Lacey likes to forget she's got a health problem, whereas we all realize we do."

"I think Lacey's a snob, and I'll be glad to be rid of her."

"Why don't I believe you?"

Jeff offered a rueful smile. " 'Cause I've always been a lousy liar." He tugged gently on Katie's hair. "You going to be okay?"

"I don't know. For a while, I was hating the

thought of leaving this place, but now, I can't wait to go. This place is making me depressed."

Jeff lifted her chin. "You're Jenny House's biggest fan. Don't change."

She shrugged. "I better get back to Chelsea. She didn't want to be alone too long. If you see Lacey—"

"I'll drag her up to your room bodily," Jeff finished.

When Katie returned, Chelsea had no news to report about the missing Lacey. By suppertime, she still hadn't returned. Katie didn't want to alarm Mr. Holloway, but she was worried about Lacey.

Chelsea lay down, yet Katie knew she didn't nap. Her breathing sounded shallow, and Katie thought she looked especially tired. Her lips had a pale bluish cast. "It's just as well that I'm going home tomorrow," Chelsea said. "I'm not feeling good."

"Should I tell someone?"

"I'll be all right until I get home, but I'll bet my doctor puts me in the hospital."

Katie's throat tightened. "Round-the-clock oxygen will be the next thing they do for you," she said.

"I don't care. I wouldn't have traded this summer here for anything." Chelsea shut her eyes. "Why doesn't Lacey come back?"

Katie longed to get her hands around Lacey's throat. No matter how Amanda's death had affected her, didn't she realize that they all needed each other? How could she have spent the entire summer at Jenny House and not have picked up that message?

Suddenly Chelsea bolted upright. "Katie! I think I know where to find Lacey."

"Tell me."

"Help me, and we'll go find her together." Chelsea's legs wobbled, and Katie put her arm around her for support.

"Do you think you should try to go anywhere?"

"Please, Katie, hurry. I'm sure I'm right."

The horses plodded up the mountain trail, with Katie leading Chelsea's mount. She continually glanced over her shoulder, anxious for her friend. Chelsea looked bad, but she'd been so determined to come, Katie had agreed to the journey. At the stables, they learned that Lacey had indeed checked out a horse around noon. Now, with the sun sinking lower in the sky, Katie felt a sense of urgency about getting to the plateau as quickly as possible.

She followed the scraps of material that Amanda had tied to the trees and found her way easily. At the crest of the ridge, she saw Lacey's horse grazing, reins tied to a tree. Katie helped Chelsea dismount, and together, they walked the rest of the way. The earth was wet, signaling that it had rained atop the mountain. The pungent smell of damp earth mingled with the scent of summer flowers.

At the very top of the ridge, the ground flattened and they discovered Lacey sitting cross-legged, staring out over the slope of mountains that nestled the waning sun. Lacey turned when she heard them approaching, but she didn't look surprised.

Katie felt a burst of angry words bubble on her

tongue, but when she and Chelsea stood beside Lacey, the words died and her anger fled. "I knew you'd come," Lacey said.

"You didn't leave us many clues. Chelsea figured it out."

Chelsea sat on the moist ground and reached for Lacey's hand. "It wasn't very hard once I started thinking about it."

"What's that?" Katie asked, pointing. For the first time, she noticed a pile of rocks laid out in the shape of a cross. At the head, there were three tall sticks standing upright and meeting at the top to form a tepee. Around the tepee, Lacey had placed a hand-twisted garland of wildflowers—wisteria and violets, Queen Anne's lace and frothy cascades of small yellow and orange blossoms. In the center, she had stuck her copy of the photo Mr. Holloway had given them.

"Everyone should have a memorial," Lacey said matter-of-factly. "This is Mandy's."

"It's beautiful," Chelsea said. "You've been planning it, haven't you?"

"I stashed my picture in the barn last week. I knew this day was coming. I'm going to leave it here."

Katie felt overwhelmed. Odd that Lacey would be the one to have thought of such a thing. "It might get ruined when it rains," she said. "Are you sure you want to leave it?"

"Of course. How else can Mandy look out over the mountains?"

Chelsea fingered the petals of the flowers. She took a tube of lipstick from her pocket and drew a bright red heart around Amanda's gamin face. "So all the fairies and elves who come here at night will know who this is for," she explained.

"I wish Amanda were here," Katie said, unable to contain her sadness any longer. "I miss her . . ."

Lacey turned to her. "We've got to make a pact with each other."

"What kind of pact?" Katie asked against the lump in her throat.

"That we'll all come here next summer and visit the memorial." Lacey's expression was one of dogged determination as she stared hard at Chelsea.

Chelsea glanced away. "That's a long way off—"

"You've got to promise me." Lacey's voice grew insistent, and her gaze shifted to Katie, her eyes glittering like blue jewels.

Katie held out her hand, palm up. "I promise," she said.

Immediately, Lacey placed her hand, palm down, on top of Katie's. Both of them looked to Chelsea. The brown-haired girl slowly inched out her hand, and Katie saw that her nail beds were blue from lack of oxygen. Silently, she begged Chelsea to be brave enough to seal the pact with her touch.

Chelsea's hand slid over Lacey's and Katie's and held firm. "I promise," she whispered.

"Then it's a deal," Lacey declared, scrambling to her feet, without sentiment. "Now, let's watch the sun set."

Katie rose beside her, and they both helped Chelsea to her feet. They stood shoulder to shoulder, facing west, where crimson rays blanketed the sky, bathing the world in red-gold splendor. The air smelled fresh and new, washed clean and scented with the sharp aroma of pine needles.

Chelsea cried, "Look!"

Above them, where the sky was still slightly blue, a rainbow arched, shimmering like colorful ribbons trapped in the light. "Amanda's looking at us," Katie told them. And at that moment, Katie knew, really knew, that Amanda had found her place over the rainbow and would not return to Kansas. She waved good-bye, and the others blew a kiss heavenward.

They each touched the memorial one more time and walked to where the horses waited. There they mounted up and rode back down the mountain to Jenny House.

Follow the continuing friendship
of the girls at Jenny House.

COMING IN FEBRUARY:

She Died Too Young, a One Last Wish novel

Chelsea's story in the continuing saga of the friends from Jenny House.

Chelsea James desperately needs a heart transplant. While waiting months for a compatible donor, she meets Jillian, who needs a heart-lung transplant. They become fast friends. And Jillian's brother, DJ, awakens feelings in Chelsea she's never known before. As her situation grows desperate, Chelsea finds herself in a contest for her life against the friend she's grown to love.

COMING IN MAY:

For All the Days of Her Life, a One Last Wish novel

Lacey's story in the continuing saga of the friends from Jenny House.

Lacey Duval hates being a diabetic. She runs with a crowd that has no understanding of sickness, and she doesn't want any of them to know about her world of insulin injections, rigid diet, and controlled exercise. But when her denial of her disease puts her life in jeopardy, Lacey must face reality and fight to live.